Twisted

Dwayne Williams

NEWMAN SPRINGS PUBLISHING
320 Broad Street
Red Bank, NJ 07701

First originally published by Newman Springs Publishing 2024

ISBN 979-8-89308-694-2 (Paperback)
ISBN 979-8-89308-695-9 (Digital)

Printed in the United States of America

RIP to Big Ron, Melvin Irving, Cocky Kyle, Tim Moore, Sabrina Patterson, Yolanda Walker, my daughter Tyesha Smith, and my baby brother Damon Williams. A special shout-out to my mother, Margaret Williams, and to the people who looked down on me and turned their backs on me, leaving me for dead.

Superior Sixty-First, my nigga Steal Bill, little Tommy.

A special shout-out to my kids: Christopher Welch, Bernice Sparks, Dwayne Smith, Calvin Hicks, and Damillion C. C. Willis my girl Rhonia from 105 much love.

Carwash Life Story

Fʀᴏᴍ ᴛʜᴇ ᴀɢᴇ ᴏꜰ ꜰɪᴠᴇ, I ɢʀᴇᴡ up without a father. I was the fourth child of my mother, and I was always told that I was the black sheep; my other sisters and brothers lived out of state with their father. Never hearing or seeing them was hard. My mother sold liquor from her home, cooked dinners, and held card games for big money. Being a mama's boy was a curse for me because that's all I knew—her telling me I was a black sheep and that she should have closed her legs at my birth. Not understanding what she was saying at the time, I stayed under her mother's wing. She kept me clean-cut and fed and taught me that the sky was the limit. I always stayed out of the way, watching *The Flintstones* and *The Jetsons*, sitting in the middle of the floor playing with Tonka trucks and army men.

I grew up on the east side of Cleveland, in the projects of E. Fifty-Fifth King Kennedy, the Browns, and Sixty-First Beauer. I would walk to school with my head held high; my mother was well-known. Looking around, there were prostitutes, pimps, gangsters shooting dice, and a lot of pill deals. At my house, there were sometimes fights, with people arguing over losing their money. My mother held it down by pulling her .38 and telling everyone to leave.

Two years passed with still no word from my sisters or brother. My mother's drinking started to get worse, and she was losing everything. The police tried to shake her down, making her pay or close it down, so we walked away with nothing, living from house to house. Different men beat her, but she always fought back. My friend, Mrs.

Peacock, took us in, letting us sleep on her hardwood floor. My mother turned into her maid, eating their scraps.

She was thirty-one years old, kept her head up, and was still a head-turner. She sent me to school, still clean-cut and fed. I remember going to centers for lunches and walking far just to stand in line for hours for free food and government cheese. My mom always prayed and cried, sometimes having nothing to eat. One day, coming home from school at Gilligan's Elementary on Cedar Eighty-First, our bags were packed, and she was sitting there with an unbreakable smile on her face. Welfare had found us a place to live; the house already had furniture, food, lights, and gas. I thought it was a God that she was praying to. My mother stopped drinking and became the mother at the same time father I knew.

A month passed, and more good news came. She was four months pregnant and about to have my baby sister. But things started going up and down, and her drinking started again. Even though her drinking started again, it wasn't a lot. My sister was born, but she never spoke of her daddy. At this time, my life started to change from watching the hustle up and down Woodland Avenue. The game started getting to me.

I started running pills from one person to another down the street, making $50 doing that going to school and $50 coming home from school. At eight years old, I was making $100 doing nothing. I kept my mouth closed, telling my mother I found a wallet in a field because I was always good at finding things. I put food on the table, helping my mom. She was never a fool.

One day, she followed me, staying behind, hiding, and watching when my pill man gave me the bag. She walked up to him, confronting him and throwing fists at him. When I got home from school, she had a washing machine cord in her hand. She ordered me to go to my room, take my clothes off, and get in the tub. That cord left welts I felt for days. My first fight was at school. Getting teased, I took a number 2 pencil and stabbed a boy in the neck with it. My mother had to come and get me. This time it was a thick belt, and the school put me out. At that point, I never cried again and learned how to take pain. They put me in Buckeye Woodland on Buckeye, but that only lasted a week before I got kicked out again for fighting. That boy's cousins jumped me.

The system kept trying, putting me in Union Elementary off of Broadway, which was another problem because it was the Whites against Blacks. Getting off the buses, they waited, throwing rocks and beer bottles at us. That was a turn-on for me and my friends. That was my life; I wanted the drama.

Now I was ten years old in the sixth grade, and loving it. My sister was now two-and-a-half, doing well, walking and talking. My mom tried her best to stay sober and keep out of jail for us kids. For a while, I stopped running pills, working by cutting grass, going to the store, and working for our landlord painting houses, making an honest living. But in June, after school got out for the summer, I was going to the store and witnessed a police chase that ended on the corner of Sixty-First and Woodland. The police shot a fourteen-year-old boy in the head, killing him. People stood around, throwing anything and everything at the police. I ran home, telling my mother and friends. But the next week, my friends wanted to see how it felt to steal a car themselves. So they did and put it in an alley. The older boys took it from them, stripped and burned it, showing us what to do.

I'm not going to lie; my mom really did try her best by keeping a tight hold on me, riding the bus with me, talking to my teacher, making me change my clothes, doing my homework, and then doing whatever she had for me to do around the house. I stayed in the front yard only to play until the streetlights came on, then came in, took a bath at eight thirty, and went to bed. My older sisters and brother came to Cleveland to visit, trying to put me in check and see our little sister. We looked alike but had no real connections. To this day, it's still the same—no connection.

The fast life was my dream; the rush turned me on. After my family left and went back to Washington, my mom's drinking got worse. She put herself into a weeklong *coma* at Metro, close to dying. Coming home from her bloody and passed out was scary. I became a man at that moment.

Her friends around the corner and the lady across the hall kept an eye on us, feeding us and making sure I stayed there watching my sister and my new baby brother. When my mom came home, she was proud of me for holding it down and keeping folks out of our lives. After making sure home was cool, my life went back to thugging. The older people had my little crew being their lookout. After school, we met at the playground, shooting ball in the daytime, and stealing cars at times. The hubcap hustle was ours—two hundred a set, a 150 being the lookout, making sure no one came around. It only took about an hour to do a whole car and burn it. The older people went to car lots, taking new cars with the keys under the floor mats—twenty cars a night; everyone *ate*. The junkyard was everything—the tires five hundred, the car itself about three thousand.

The first time I ever drove a car, I had to sit on phone books, the seat close to the steering wheel, coming down Woodland Avenue. My mom heard from her friends that they saw me drive. That belt became my friend again—no pain, no tears. My pride had to stay strong. After that, I started drinking myself. I passed out in an open, empty field with tall grass. My clothes were funky from throwing up, but that belt was my friend. Once again, I said that I was a man and ran away from home, climbing into my girlfriend's window. We were eleven years old now. Her mom liked me and even wanted me for herself. Truthfully, I was into older women. Back then, age wasn't a number. Besides, everyone smoked weed and drank. My close friend was a screwdriver in a sock full of marbles. I even stole my teacher's car because she told my mother that I didn't come to school.

The hood kept quiet; the police couldn't prove it. My crew was at it, putting in work, going everywhere, and coming back to the hood paid. Other crews came down, taking from us. That's how the gangs BCO, KKO, the DDs, and others formed. It turned into a citywide thing—fighting, stealing, breaking into everything, busting, and snatching from Randall Mall, Higbee's Downtown Tower City. We even took Bob Evan's meat trucks and beer trucks but never killed people with guns like now. We fought one-on-one, shook hands, drank Boone's Farm or some Irish Rose, and went on about our business. We even did break dancing and spray-painted walls, buses, and trains. The police and the feds raided every street corner, taking everyone to jail and juvenile centers, and making headlines.

A lot of us went to court and were returned home to our mothers. I had over fifteen grand thefts, two breaking and entering charges, and truancy. I was given six months detention, the first eleven-year-old to order time in the hood. They kept me away from the older sections. Fights broke out, and I never had any visits or mail, which made me want a life of crime even more, not caring.

I got out on May 6, 1982, at the age of twelve and a half. Mom had found Grandma and Uncle, who were into after-hours business and drug use, but they got on my case, though it still didn't help. They lived on Lakeview on Timelert. I started back stealing cars, taking them out of people's driveways, breaking the gearstick, and pushing them down the street. Then we popped the pin and went about our business.

I had an empty warehouse on Beauer where we took the motors, transmissions, seats, front ends, and doors out of cars. The rest of the car we pushed down the street, letting the police tow them away. At the age of twelve, thousands of dollars were made. We even used big U-Haul trucks with air tools. We hit Spencer's Buick on Buckeye and Quaker's Buick. They had every car that was money—Cadillacs, '98s, Chevy Impalas, and Novas. We had so many flipped cars with titles; it was crazy. Hell, after six months, we even sold them back for a good few hundred dollars. On our time off, we hit game rooms, laundromats, and restaurants. Money was made. The police and the feds were going crazy because all the older guys were locked up doing time, and my crew got bigger and smarter. Mom was doing her thing, letting go since we needed a hangout to chill and drink. Mr. B's on Fifty-Fifth wouldn't let us kick it—"Too young," he said.

So we made the neighborhood game room our game room. We used the door to get in. That's where we shot dice, smoked weed, drank beer, and skipped school. The owner was cool; just put money in his pocket. Hell, he even sold us guns. The feds found our warehouse, taking everything. Fingerprints were found as well.

Secret indictments and warrants had the police kicking in doors at three to six in the morning. My mom took a pastor to get me baptized, thinking that might save me. Rev. Black's family were thugs too. He had a corner store with games in it. By my name being in the streets as a leader of a car thief crew, I was the one who broke into his store. He and his family surrounded my house, kicking in the door, and looking for me with guns. People started pulling out guns on my mom when she walked down the street, looking for me. My mom, sister, and baby brother were getting pulled up because of my shit. Damn, now I was in too deep. At twelve and a half years old, I was wanted dead or alive, so I laid low, thinking of going to school, going back to the center with my mom, and getting that free lunch.

One day, people told us a white Cadillac with two White dudes was parked on the corner, looking down my street. Not taking it too seriously, we walked up to our house. A bomb went off, blowing up our house. We got out of the way just in time, lying in the tall grass next door in a field. At that point, we left and moved to my grandma's house, getting out of the hood. But over at Granny's house, I had buried $15,000 and two .38 snub noses in her backyard for my mom's fresh start.

Now I had Granny and seventeen uncles and aunts on my ass for putting my family in danger. Three of my uncles were gangsters: Johnny, Kenny Shields, who was a Black Panther, and my uncle Junebug, who had the biggest hands. They got on my case but it still didn't stop me. My cousins thought I was crazy; everyone did. I ran away, hiding in Garden Valley. I had a thirty-year-old woman who had her own place. Stealing cars was back in place. Shortly after, on 116th, they had a Sugarhill free concert at Woodhill Park. Everyone was there—the DDs, BCOs, D30s, MOs. A large fight broke out. People were running everywhere. Blood was seen on people's faces and clothes. Gunshots were fired. My legs were hit; a bullet hit my shin. I tried my best to run. I got to my car and went back to Lakeview to my mom. My uncle took my car down the street and burned it.

My granny, mom, and aunts cried, thinking I was going to die. I lost a lot of blood. Mom took a sewing needle and some gin, made me drink some, and used the rest on my wound, sewing up my shin. I recovered about two weeks later. It was hard to walk, so I laid low, kicking it with my cousins, and getting to know them. They were wild too, mostly into girls, nothing like me. It was weird being around them because they were mama's boys. My mom and granny had enough of my shit, so they took me down to the DH on Twenty-Second, locking me up, saying it was my time and to save my life. Everybody from down the way was there. Over 250 people knew me and my crew.

Two years later, I went to court. I had over twenty-two counts of grand theft auto, twenty-two counts of receiving stolen property, four counts of truancy, and three counts of breaking and entering. Mom was there. I was sitting in handcuffs and shackles on my ankles, in a bright-orange suit, thinking I was coming home. Judge Rocca issued me a sentence of six months to twenty-one years. I rode out a week later. I was ordered to go to Cuyahoga Hills. It was June 6, 1982. I was there for eighteen months, fighting and wilding out. I was ordered to go to Hudson. There, I was for two and a half years. After calming down and doing what I had to do, I was granted a group home in Elyria, Ohio, for two years. The street life was leaving my life. I started going to school, learning, and doing what I was told. I never heard anything else from anyone in my family. I was left for dead from the day I was sentenced.

Being locked up, I witnessed beatings, murders, and rapes. The COs were fucked up. It was their way or no way. There were a lot of riots. People went to Charity Hospital for cracked heads and rape. A lot never made it back. Over ten people raped one boy, mostly White boys. My first love was going to AB Hart Junior High. Some girls jumped her, killing her by stabbing her in her vagina because she was still in love with me. Her brother was locked up with me for a short time. Hearing that, I went crazy. I had on my plate my family not keeping in touch and staying alive in there. It was a prison for kids.

But after being in the group home and doing a lot better, the state found my mom and let us visit. I was going home on weekends. Mom had gotten her life back together. My baby sister and brother were in school now. She had found a small house off Wade Park Blaine. My sister was, I believe, six years old, and my brother was about four. I think my sister was riding a school bus. She wore pop-bottle glasses. The kids teased and hit her, my mom said. So I went to her bus stop. When it came, dropping her off, she was happy as hell seeing her big brother. The kids who teased her I beat up real bad. The bus driver shook my hand after, saying my sister was a good girl. I thanked him and we left. The other kids on the bus were in shock, and people on my mother's street were too because they thought I was just a make-believe story that was told. My mother stood proudly in the street with a big smile, telling me, "Boy, get your ass in the house." My caseworker was in disbelief at what she had just witnessed. Even she said I was right for protecting my family. Rumors spread quickly in her new neighborhood.

My cousin, my age, lived around the corner; he went to Martin Luther King High School. He had hands, but he wasn't my breed. He was a mama's boy anyway. He had heard I was coming home and waited with open arms. My sister never had any problems again. Matter of fact, the girls whom I beat up, who were the school bullies, had crushes on me.

Car stealing was now out of my life. I started turning into a square type of dude, being trusted again. Mom wanted me back around. I felt the love. Granny missed me and wanted me home. She wanted me to come and live with her. Granny was getting sick. My uncles and aunts were too deep into that drug life. My mom said no.

Keeping secrets, they never knew about the truth of my aunt and older girl cousin sexually abusing me and my best friend's daughter teaching me how to eat pussy. I can still remember the feelings and nasty taste of it, the hairs going inside my mouth. But doing that made me want older women.

I had a thirty-year-old woman still in Garden Valley who was crazy about me. She had bought me new clothes and shoes to come home to with a few hundred dollars. My boys gave me a Buick Regal, power blue, a deep blue ragtop with the brains blown out, with a gold nose, bucket seats, chrome rims, and last but not least, trues and Vogues with sounds. After going to reviews in court, they finally granted me a month's visit home and determined I was not a menace to society. So on June 7, 1987, I started to come home from the kid prison system.

When I came home, my cousin and his friends, dogs off Superior, welcomed me home with a block party. The choice of any big booty was given. I remember hearing Too Short, Keith Sweat, and NWA, watching my cousin and them smoking and selling weed. The hustle was laid-back. I got in the game, making $1,000 a night. Within thirty days, I had money, my Buick, and three big booties with two trap houses for my weed sales. My money was hidden in my mom's basement floor—$13, 850 two pounds. They went to my girls to keep flipping for me while I was gone. After I turned eighteen years old, I was good to go. I was on my way. Period. In 1989, it was all over. I am a free me.

Mom had to sit me down, letting me know that there were different people, places, and things out there, and she gave my chrome .38 snub nose back. She also reminded me of our past—the police chase, the invaders, my friends getting killed by police, my nigga's brains off my arm and neck, those cold nights eating popcorn for the whole winter with no lights or gas. It was one or the other—sleeping on the hard floors, eating people's scraps, and the free food centers. I just hugged her as tight as I could and gave her $4,000, with tears rolling down my sad face, saying, "Never again, Mom. Your son is home."

My big booty girl had me set up with a new trap house with ten prostitutes and three money-getting gay men who dressed like women. They all wanted and needed a daddy. I was made and chosen, selling pounds and pimping once again. I was a *playa's* dream, unstoppable. I had Euclid, Prospect, and still Fifty-Fifth on lock. At eighteen years old, I had my Buick and a 1989 Fleetwood four-door Cadillac, custom-made snakeskin shoes, gator shoes, and silk sets. I was made.

The only thing Shorty wanted was my tongue and respect and our daughter. She had the prettiest mixed baby on the east side. We agreed on giving her to her mother and buying her mother a nice, peaceful home out of town, out of sight, out of mind. So Detroit was where she wanted to go. We even bought a small storefront, selling dinners. She did well, putting our daughter in school and out of the way. But Shorty and I started selling crack and weed. The weed was hers, and the girls went with her as well. Two different lives. I was on Wade Park Plaza hustling fifty-cent hits to whatever you wanted, making $1,000 to $5,000 from 8:00 a.m. to 3:00 p.m. We changed shifts—four days on and three off. We all were committed, putting in $25 a day for bond money. The vice hated the hood. We respected old people and children being around. I had the game on lock. We even bought the hood kids' popsicle trucks. Everyone was welcome.

All kids, just as long as we knew that they went to school. Shorty, with her crazy ass, loved old people and kids, so the rule was if we sold drugs in the hood, we had to take care of the hood. We bought popsicle trucks for kids. She even started a cleanup feed-me-back day for the hood, only buying everything from 105th Chicken Restaurant Abbott's every day. She had us go and buy every old piece of chicken and Polish boys that they had and had DJ Hillary play music in the parking lot of the projects all day with no drug sales or use. And this was every day of the week. She loved to give back. Even though thousands were being made, we bought from one, and that one kept love in the hood. My mom stopped letting me in her house and accepting money from me, so I turned to my baby sister and brother, saying that they found it at the store or at the playground.

My oldest sister and my newborn nephew had just moved in with my mother. Now she was twenty-two. Her birthday was on October 15, 1965. My birthday is on October 18, 1971. That's crazy, right? But listen, my little sister's birthday is March 12, 1975. My baby brother's birthday is March 15, 1977. My oldest brother's birthday is June 12, 1963.

My second sister's birthday is May 6, 1964, but I'm the black sheep of the family still to this day. I played the man of the house since I was little, and I will stay that way—the wild child. So I gave my mom $2,000 to help out this time, and she took it with no problem and told me to leave. Wow, that's cool. I kept my eye on my sister because she was not off the press. Two weeks after her being there, she was already down the street with a backyard mechanic who had too much traffic and stolen parts, but he and she were seeing each other. He wanted to have sex; she didn't. He tried to take it. I heard about it from the hood, so I took my cousin, my sportsman

12-gauge, and put him at the bottom of the street on his knees at ten thirty in the morning. I put it in his mouth. My mother came running, crying in her underwear, begging me not to kill him. I busted the top of his head. My mother took the gun, and I walked away saying, "You won't be that lucky next time. I will kill you." My cousin was afraid for him too, knowing that I really wanted to kill him. My sister never met me or knew of my ways. She learned real quick, but after that, she and he remained seeing each other, and now she had four kids with him.

A little bit after that day, someone who was hanging around had stolen some real shit from them, thinking it was me. They caught me with my *pants* down, asleep at my mother's house. They jumped me, pistol-whipped me, and put me in a truck, taking me to Euclid Seventy-Fourth. They jumped me a lot worse and left me for dead. I lay there for about two days, and I climbed back to Blaine to my mother's house. From there, my mother got me back to health. My sister had it out with him after I busted his head with the gun. I got my cousin and six of his friends; we set the house on fire, making whoever was in there come out. We shot up everyone. My sister lived; she got shot in the leg. My cousin and his friends walked away slowly in different ways. I walked down the street; the neighbors watched in fear. No one said anything to the police. I made off because I climbed up in a tall tree, looking down at the whole scene. The neighbors went back into their houses and never opened their doors. After a while, everything went back to normal. They said he had it coming to him anyway. People even started shaking my hand, saying, "You're the man."

My new crew was young and crazy like me. We started making more money. People stayed out of our way when we walked down the street, opening up doors for us. But I ended up getting caught for drug sales and was sentenced to sixteen months in Lancaster prison. At nineteen years old, I was going to a real-life prison. Getting off the Bluebird, four body bags were getting on the bus. I was thinking, *Really?* Looking around the yard, niggas' chests were bigger than my head, their arms too. Being amazed by all that I was seeing, believe it or not, it was a turn-on for my drama.

I got to my pod; guys looked crazy until one dude walked up and asked, "Your name Snoop from Wade Park?"

I said, "Why?" with hard-ass brass.

"You are made. I got your back 'cause your cousin is my real nigga." So it was on just that quick. Food boxes hit my bunk. It was more Superior Sixty-Sixth Boys and Wade Park E. Thirtieth in there than it was in the streets. It was laid-back being in there, really, like it was in juvenile. But the difference was the COs' women were hustling sex for money. When people visit, they could have street food and money in their pockets. It was wide open like that, all drugs on board, and the inmates fucking the sheep and cows on the farms here. One dude got his licked off.

At night, the lifers did their thing doing boys. Time started to ride by, writing home, hearing from the house. Things started getting crazy. The police and the feds were hitting everyone, my crew too. We got robbed for everything. What goes around comes around. Even my girl Shorty's click—it was completely over, and she moved out, which was cold. I was on my way out in about sixty days. It would still be summertime, getting prophesied out.

It was May 6, 1991, a hot day. Seventy-five dollars gate pay. On my way, the air was so fresh. Even people's clothes and styles were a lot different, the cars too. Wow, it was that quick. I don't know why butterflies hit my stomach hard. The one-and-a-half-hour ride was the longest ride ever. Handshakes and hugs were crazy.

Mom had moved to a bigger and better house. Mom didn't play company in her house, especially my type of friends, but she fixed me fried chicken wings, buffalo fish, and salad. I already had a new pair of shoes and a new set of clothes waiting. Now it was time to hit the block. My crew had set up a party for me at Cross's Bar on Seventy-Ninth on Wade Park. I had two strippers dancing, who later fucked my brains out. That was real. From listening to everyone, they had been broken for some time. I had to do something. I did.

I went to Lander's on Cargina and got a live order to rob a buddy who had just come into town with $150,000 and keys of heroin, sitting with this shit on Wade Park under everybody's nose. I took the order. They wanted the heroin only; the money was ours. So we went and laid on the move, taking a loft ladder to the second-floor porch. We made sure no one was there by watching him and his wife and two kids ride off. So we went in, looking everywhere. We had to wait for eight hours. When they walked in the house, we put the guns on the dude, making his family sit down, tied up, duct tape over their mouths. We made him show where the money and dope were. He wouldn't tell. We made his wife stand in the middle of the floor, taking her clothes off, feeling all over her naked body, playing with her pussy, and he still wouldn't tell. Time was going by quickly. No one lived downstairs, which was good, and an empty house was next door. All this in front of the kids. So we stripped him down, beating and pistol-whipping him, blood everywhere. My dude took a broomstick and put it up his ass as hard as he could. He finally told. All along, it was in the front door frame.

So we put everything in a black bookbag, taking his four-year-old son with us to ensure our getaway. We jumped in a stolen truck, leaving his son there on the corner of his house. We went back to Lancer's Motel where our dude was. He gave us a bonus of $10,000 and said, "Stay low until I call you for the coast is clear." We did. We went out to Brook Park by the airport hotel. The dude and his family packed up and left town. They went back somewhere in Youngstown. We got four birds from our dude's people. It was raw as hell, making triple our money, putting Wade Park on their feet. It was heaven. Even the crackheads were hustling. The police and feds left the scene. While I was in prison, my other niggas got out, getting put on their feet too. Everyone was eating well.

I had to move away from Mom's house to keep them safe and stop contact with them because other hoods were coming down hard, killing everyone, robbing them, and kicking in doors day and night. There were fourteen murders in our hood alone in one month. We had to set up trap houses for all of us to live in, watching each other's backs. Even people's baby moms and mothers were getting robbed. Later, we found out it was a strong hit from California; the Crips were hitting us hard. They were hitting us in Wade Park, Hough, and Superior, and some parts of 105th. Someone made a call, breaking everyone's pockets, and closing the hood down. We took a big loss as well—$120,000 and six keys—and lost lives. My crew got hit, three dead.

While I was coming out of my new girl's house at 7:30 a.m., three guys pulled a 12-gauge shotgun to my head with her watching from the window. They took my car and my money. The car had a half-cooked key. That broke me. What's left to do? I shut everything down. I had just a few thousand in the streets. I collected quickly and went out of town myself. Everything turned deadly overnight. My mom and family remained cool, thank the Lord for that, but for everyone else, it was rough. People lost their minds because of the deaths of their loved ones. Crack and homelessness turned real. I was drinking myself like crazy. So I got a connection in Detroit. They liked me and gave me a deal with what I had in my pocket. I took a key back to Cleveland, hustling quietly, putting new people on. This time it was working better.

I thought it had lasted just long enough for us to re-up on a smaller pack because people were getting their families out. I had to leave everyone alone and go solo—me against the hood. People were hating. I had a mixed girl, a nice regal, new clothes, and money to play with.

At twenty-two years old, life was good. Until one day, my girl walked to the plaza to get some steak and eggs and some orange juice. The pavement made her fall on her ass, tearing her shirt off. I went crazy with my 9 mm. I walked up to him, beating him down. As I walked away, he started shooting at me, so we had a shootout. I ended up getting hit twice, in the leg and arm. Everyone saw what happened but never said anything, nor did he.

We had to lie low once again, stopping my hustle. So Boo and I went out to Lorain, Ohio, having a good time. The dude I shot left the hood and was never seen again. My girl was having my baby. I didn't know she was two months pregnant until that day. We were all kicking it, drinking, and listening to loud music at my cousin's house in the projects on Wade Park. All the girls were upstairs, and the boys were in the parking lot. Some dude walked up with a police special seven-shot 12. I gave him six 20 rocks for it. I was playing with it, shooting it. I heard everyone saying, "Drop it, and don't look around." Saying "Don't" means to do so. I turned around, my finger on the trigger. I shot. The driver never got out.

The passenger cop got out, blasting something loud. Everyone screamed and cried. My girl started bleeding, about to lose our child. I ran across the lot into an empty building. The police were on my ass. Brick dust was behind me from wherever. He was aiming at my head mostly. I started shooting over my shoulder at the same time, running for my life. On the side of me were kids out of nowhere, I guess on the floor that I was on. I was out of bullets, crossing the street, Crawford into Martin King Blvd, on a hill where there was a construction hole with leaves in it. That's where I hid for a while. Day police and dogs were all over me, walking on my body and face. I guess they were afraid to, but they never found me. I guess that was God's doing.

My mother came crying with my family, even my sister whom I shot. She was even crying for me. My girl was rushed to the doctor. After that, she left me and was never seen or heard from. It was dark as hell. Everybody was gone, the police too, but they were still riding the hood looking for me. So I went upstairs to my cousin's house and waited until early morning to leave. I had to buy some old clothes from crackheads to walk down the street. I went to St. Clair, hiding out, but my cousin told me everything. The police found my shotgun with my prints and who I was. The driver had a white sheet on her.

He said that there were over one hundred police looking with guns everywhere, and the ghetto bird was over my head looking. I was thinking, *Wow*. But no arrest came from that. After lying low for over twelve hours in a hole, I climbed out slowly. Looking around from down the street, I could hear the brakes and see the spotlights still looking around. I took a deep breath and ran as fast as I could into my cousin's building, up the stairs into his house.

My uncle was drunk, asleep on the couch. My cousin was drinking some Old E, saying, "Bitch, you hot, crazy. You killed that police lady." He brought some clothes from a crackhead. My mother lived down the other end of Ansel. Early that morning, I had to go back into the creek so the police couldn't follow my trail. I made it up to St. Clair Ninety-Ninth. There was a corner store that had a payphone. For some reason, I kept this junkman's number. He said that he was renting rooms and told me to come through. He got me. I walked down the tracks until I made it to his house, not knowing the horror people.

At this time, anything was perfect. It was a junkman's house. It smelled like a drunk house, basically a bando. He charged me $200 a month. I paid him. So we kicked it, drinking some store-bought vodka. A lot of different people started to come over with drinks and looking for crack, so I sold what I had. Now that life was over.

Early the next morning, I had to go and get some new clothes. The store was on 105th. On my way back, getting off the bus, there was a deep crowd of Bloods and Crips fighting. I got jumped badly. I had two black eyes, two broken ribs, and a broken leg, so now I had to lie down and heal. I kept in touch with my family at my mother's house. I kept a 12-gauge on my mom's floor on the third floor in my old room. My sister was getting picked on by some girls around the corner in a group home. My older sister went and fought them, but they kept it up.

The police were looking for me still, but the heat of it started to fade away. But I still had to watch my back. My landlord on St. Clair didn't know anything about this, or the other murders and shootouts. One day I called my mother. For once in her life, she said she needed to take care of a problem. So I flew like a bird getting there. People who knew me were like, "Damn, it's on now. Dwayne is coming down the street." My mother and her friend were standing on her porch, Mom smiling from ear to ear. She quickly walked away. My sister, baby sister, and brother ran out to hug me, saying they missed me and told me what was going on. I went in to eat so Mom wouldn't see me go upstairs to get my 12-gauge. No one knew it was there. Being who I was, I got it, put shells in, and came down the stairs out the front door. I walked up to their house.

There were around twenty girls in the yard and sitting on the porch. So I asked, "Who is picking on my baby sister?" Just at this time, my family had come around the corner trying to stop me from shooting. I asked my sister, "Who is it?"

She said, "All of them." I shot in the air once. They ran into the house screaming for help. I shot six times through the windows and door. We all walked away, me back in the woods across the street from Mom's front door. That was the neighborhood talk, but after that, no more messing with my family happened. Mom said the police came looking with search warrants and said, "If we find him, he's dead."

Mom said with a smile, "You don't know my son. Trust me." She had me laughing my ass off because she was right. It was too late to turn back, and I didn't know myself either.

I walked through the woods down the creek, thinking of a new nickname. My name Snoop was dead and gone. I put my 12-gauge by this old tree. I buried it in a shallow spot, easy to get to. On St. Clair, I waited for the bus, no police. The hood was funny like that. The bus came. While I was getting to the house, the old man was there. We talked. I told him that I needed a new name and a different lifestyle. People were asking who I was and where I came from. He said, "My son and I were out of town, and you come live with me." At this time, I was nineteen years old. So that was what we did—father and son—which, at the time, I really needed. We went scraping every morning, fishing, and having father-and-son time. His real sons accepted me right away as their stepbrother. But no one ever knew of my past and never asked. Learning how to hustle differently was turning me around.

They threw me a party. Everyone they knew was there and had a stripper who could take an ice tray in her pussy with the fattest ass a man could see and touch. He told everyone that I had just come home from jail. Everyone paid money to watch me fuck the stripper in the middle of the floor. I said, "No, hell no, my name is Dwayne." The next morning, the neighborhood started calling me Chicken Wayne. I started answering to it, so that was my new nickname. Respect was there from everyone because the old man was a Golden Gloves boxer who had mad hands. I learned how to paint houses, cut grass, detail cars, cook ribs, and clean out houses. I learned these types of hustles; the police were mad as hell because I was hiding right under their noses. Believe it or not, I was even getting welfare with my real name.

People started liking me, letting me cut their grass, take out their trash, and even go to the store for them. A few dollars kept the pain away. Even the store owner was letting me do things for them. A man on our street took me under his wing, painting houses, and plumbing work. Thinking about that stripper, she had fallen into AIDS. Later, she got killed behind our house in the field, naked with her throat cut.

There was a pretty girl who lived across the street. She was around the corner at the YMCA. She had the smile, the booty, and the light voice that had me gone, but not good enough, not knowing because of what was going on in my house. It was a turnoff. Gay people were coming over; the old man was both. Everything went—an open house. It became the house of the town. Wild sex parties, drug deals in and out all day and night.

While selling drugs, I was starting to smoke Primos. Trying to get away was hard because the police were looking for me harder. This lifestyle was now the only life that I knew—having sex with every prostitute who walked on St. Clair and came over. Even with gay dudes, play-to-pay secrets were well-kept on my part.

Later, my sister started calling me again, saying I needed to do something because my kids were going through some shit. I needed to get a job and a house. So I started working for a temp place named Kelly Services, getting up to $500 a week. I let my family pick it up every Friday for my kids. That lasted for four months. Getting high stopped after her call. My other hustle kept going. I even got in cool with the salt mine down the street, picking up rock salt and trash cans full for people's driveways for $50 a can.

At twenty-one years old, I thought I was unstoppable. I was a street hustler's dream, getting paid without selling drugs. That was the life. Sometimes I washed twenty cars a day, $10 per car, and cut twenty yards a day, $20 per yard. That was the life, I thought. People trusted me and looked up to me for my kind of hustle, having relationships with women who had real jobs and wanted me for them. Everything was going well for once in my life.

One Tuesday morning, I was at work and got a phone call that my mother had been rushed to the hospital for diabetes. Mom was coming home but needed money for the phone at home. I had the money to pay the bill. My sister, who had never smoked weed before, smoked weed with her friend and Mom at home on the porch. I gave Mom $500. My sister didn't know this. She came talking big shit, so we started fighting. It went into the middle of the street. It was Mike Tyson and Holyfield. People sat and watched, cheering us on, killing each other for hours. Black eyes and busted nose—that was me. Her, just a busted lip. I taught her good. My mother didn't say anything about the money I gave her. After that, I went to the store, and got my beer and her wine. I passed out on the floor. I was woken up handcuffed, and fifteen police surrounded me, taking me to jail for DUI. She told the police everything about the murders, but the system was shut down that day I went to court, so they were forced to let me go. They knew they had me.

After that, I went back to the hood, St. Clair, doing my thing and not looking back. Coming home, I had a cookout and my first threesome. People treated me like I was a star. I was still watching my back because I had to use a new address for cover. Time went on; everything turned normal. Cases went unsolved.

It was a man and his girl, me, the old man, his brother, the dude's sister, the old man's girlfriend, and two other brothers living in this house. Fights were everyday occurrences from getting drunk, and the old man's play brother was there as well.

One night, my dude went to work, leaving his girl there. They all wanted to fuck her, but she wouldn't give in. They got her drunk until she passed out cold. Twenty of them ran a train on her. She woke up being raped, and about ten more dudes were in line having their way. The police came, taking everyone to jail except for me and the old lady. Charges were never filed because they all got out. She and her sister never said anything to her dude about what happened. If he had said anything, they would have jumped him and left him for dead like everyone who crossed their path.

The old man and his friend went out looking for some young play and came home with a young dude who had a drinking and weed problem. They went downstairs, closing the door, keeping everyone from coming in to see what was going on. Music was loud all night, and I could hear them talking about whose turn it was next. The boy must have wanted out because they said he pulled a .38 handgun and shot himself in the head. The gunshot could be heard all the way down the street. Everyone ran to the house at the same time. Everyone in the house ran out, saying that he killed himself. I was the first one to go in, seeing the boy lying in the middle of the floor with his brains out. He had on some new Jordans.

I took them and checked his pockets, getting out the $200 they had paid him for sex, I guess. I went for the gun but decided to leave it there. The police came; people were all on the street, tripping on what had gone on in the house, saying real crazy shit. Since he was my age, I went down for questioning with everyone else, but I had to go down again. They never asked about my past at Wade Park. Butterflies? Hell yeah. Once again, everyone got out. I heard that the boy was homeless, living with his mother and baby brother in their car on Platt.

My hustle went weak for a while. The old man, I guess, started having some type of feeling for me, making me let him suck me down and have sex with him while the old lady watched. If I had said anything about it, he would kill me and her. He even tried to take my money, getting high smoking crack with his friends. If I tried to leave, he would find me and kill me. Shit was crazy. But by the grace of God, or just the neighborhood wanting to shut down the house, it happened. The police and sheriffs came around seven in the morning, kicking in the door, and putting everyone out in five minutes. They boarded up every window and padlocked each door. With nowhere to go and no money, I was happy. Seven years of this shit, and at twenty-five now, I ended up going to prison for a drug case from '92. The judge gave me one year, so I ended up down in Lancaster.

Coming home, I went back to St. Clair, living on the same street, 110th, with someone else, which didn't last too long. From her house to another girl's house, it was like that until child support cases popped up. Now Lorain County was taking me in for felony child support. I went back to prison for six months. Now St. Clair was dead to me, so I went and applied for CMAA and got it ASAP for my birthday; I was twenty-six years old.

Going backward to my old hood, the projects at 5101 Quincy Avenue, I moved in on my birthday. Wow. It was a gift. I had no TV, no nothing, and was sleeping on the hard-ass floor. I even had to go to free centers to eat. Everyone had turned their backs on me, all besides two sisters who still lived on St. Clair.

I had no other choice but to go to work at Mr. Magic on Cedar and hustle again, not looking back on the past. But this time, the past had made me even stronger. I started eating like the game was made to be—money over bitches and problems and no friends. The family talk, Mom called sometimes, letting me know what's what. That's how I learned that my baby brother was selling crack on Eighty-Eighth. He got caught up in a police chase and went to jail with crack and a 9 mm on him. I was hurt more than anything because he only had six more months left in junior college with my baby sister. I went to Mom's house back in Wade Park.

I sat and talked with Mom, drinking some beer, thinking what I could do to save him from fucking up his life. I got two of my dudes who were wild like me. We went to the police station. I talked to a chief of police, a lady cop who knew my past real well. So we made a deal to clear his record. I had to take his cases, and he was free. I went in, and he went home with my two dudes. The following week, I was home, but I had a PO officer to report to, which was good. I went back to the project, making and having bodyguards watching every-thing that moved around me. I did not know that the police had come in, putting bugs in my house and sending in undercovers with marked money. The undercovers were the crackheads I was dealing crack to. Some wild-ass shit, huh?

I had no other choice but to shut shit down and chill. My pock-ets were full. We exchanged mostly all the big bills, taking a small loss, but that's part of the game. Hell, I had over $100,000. Mom called me, saying that a dude from St. Clair who was gay was coming to her house, looking for me for whatever reason. He never left his number. I didn't know anyway. He and my baby brother were sup-posed to be looking for me.

The dude said he had a job for me. Instead, he gave the job to my brother. After work, they hang out in Garden Valley, a place where they kill first and ask questions later. My brother wasn't gay at all; it was just work. The gay dude had a spot there to hide for some of his phony shit. Anyway, he loved the shit out of weed and was a Blood. He had hands better than mine; he would fight anybody, anywhere. Besides, he had cousins who lived on Kinsman, up the street from where they were. But like in Cleveland, you get niggas who hang out at the corner store and on the corners. Some said that my brother got cool with a few of them, smoking weed. But that was a good setup to get them in the apartment that my brother and the gay dude were in.

Not taking long, their plan worked. They shot the gay dude in the face nine times, and my brother twice in the back. The gay dude was in the back bedroom with no face, blood everywhere, and my brother was at the door, dying from his own blood. All the windows were down, the heat was on blast, and it was June 12, 1996. When I found their bodies, a cousin who lived up the street came and saw my brother. Hearing him asking for help softly, he just left him.

My brother's disappearance was on the news. He was missing for two weeks in that heat. On June 12, that day, me and my girls from St. Clair kicked that door in. He was on the other side of it, falling apart in my hands. I went outside that apartment; no one was seen anywhere. I shot seventeen times in the air. I threw about $15,000 on the ground for the reward of the people who did this to him. Not knowing that they were watching out their deep, dark screen windows. Now believe this, they were afraid for their life and turned themselves in to the police. Only one was sentenced to life in Marion prison, where Wade Park was waiting on the dude and my brother's cousins. They made him their bitch. After two years, the dude was found dead in his cell, hanging. What's crazy was my family thought it was because of that fight with my baby sister.

And they had jumped me because they thought I had something to do with his death. At the same time, I had my three-year-old daughter in my life with my other four kids. My family was keeping them on the down low because their mother was smoking crack really badly, bringing different dudes into her house, and having sex for crack.

My daughter had a cold and wanted some attention, some love. She kept crying. My kids said that a dude was there saying if she couldn't stop her from crying, he would leave. There was a bucket of mop water in the kitchen where they were. She took my daughter's face and submerged it, killing her. Between my brother's stress and now my daughter's death, I went back to the projects, drinking heavily and smoking a lot of crack, losing my mind.

I put a fully loaded nine to my head, trying to end my life. It felt like someone was taking the gun from me. I pointed the gun at the wall, and it went off, unloading completely. I sat there tripping, like, wow, damn, for real. I could have killed myself. Still feeling like the world was closing in on me, I had no other choice but to get some serious help.

I went to the Salvation Army on Fifty-Fifth, around the corner from me. While I was there, I knew that I had a secret indictment for those drug deals and marked money. I lost my house, and the police came to get me from rehab. I went to prison for one year. Once again, no letters or visits, just state pay and coming home with nowhere to live. When the police hit my house, they found $82,000 in my couch. The rest of everything, crackheads had fun wearing my clothes. My year was up, and I went back to the Salvation Army. They welcomed me with open arms. I found a place in East Cleveland, Terrance Tower, apartment 1214.

Now I was about twenty-nine years old, still wild as hell, not knowing anyone, with no money again, sleeping on the floor with roaches, with everyone watching my every move. So I started doing shit, walking around, working at the corner car wash for $50 a day. Doing that opened up the door to meet other hustlers, which were Folks and Crips. Now getting back on my feet, and keeping people out of my apartment, I even moved in with a girl who lived downstairs on the eighth floor. That was the crack house and free pussy, fucking every crackhead in the building.

Now my name started ringing bells. The dudes were hating me because I was getting money and fucking better than them. I stayed in fights in until one day I went to a hood bar for a few beers. The owners were my baby sister's family, which was my family now. East Cleveland couldn't stop me. Now I was hanging out on Taylor and Noble, doing all-nighters, still different pussy every night. Living in East Cleveland was a completely different world. The police were thugs. They would pull up wanting you to run so they could shoot you. If you didn't run, they would take your money and leave your hustle, so your hustle could keep going until the next time. People lived in empty homes with lights, gas, and water on, like it was okay to do. They never said shit about anything or never came when you needed them.

I witnessed a lot of murders and rapes that the police committed against streetwalkers who wouldn't sell ass for them. Robberies from hustlers to hustlers, setups were crazy from the streetwalkers. The free food centers were filled with crackheads and drunks. People were so bad that they were selling their food for crack. Life in East Cleveland was just like after hours—you could buy beer. After a while, I stayed out of the way and stopped hustling, going back to work out on Mayfield Rd. I worked nights at Burger King for $8.75 an hour.

Doing that, I met a girl, and we lived together and had a baby boy. She lived in the Broadway Fleet area but was crazy as hell about her mother. I knew her from the projects, and I was older than she was. She had just finished high school, and I was in my thirties. Her mom hated me but loved what I could do for her. A father to my son, I always made the best for him. I even went to prison for breaking and entering; doing so, for two years. As soon as I went to jail, she had another dude in her bed. I put her in school to be a nurse. I bought her a car before I had one, taking her and her family on trips out of town, doing what a real man is supposed to do, only to learn that the baby wasn't mine, so her family said. I was in love with her young ass, something that I never thought could happen.

Going through shit with her and her family pushed me back, looking for someone else. I can't believe how God works. My oldest son's mother lived in her hood and never lost love for me, wanted me back. My son needed me anyway. Now my life was complete. I left the streets alone, worked, and stayed in the house, which made us happy like a family should be until one day, her sister moved in with us. She was a drunk with a body that she didn't mind sharing. We stayed on the low for a while until she wanted me to herself. I said hell no. She told me everything, thinking that would make me and my woman break up. It only made it better. Now we were having mad threesomes, the best ever, two sisters. But it was hard to keep this away from our son. He was nine years old, and smart as hell. He said that he heard us one day. Explaining something like that to a kid was difficult. He said that he was aware of my past, being in the streets. He said there was a kid who went to his school that looked and acted like him. What? And they were two years apart. Wow! My mind was blown.

So the next day, I went to school with him, talking to his mommy on the phone. She was tripping now because she wanted to know the truth. I saw a woman that I had a small relationship with. She said, "Hi, Dwayne."

My son said, "That's the boy's mother."

His mother heard everything. The boy's mother asked, "Are you here to see your son, Dwayne Jr.?" The boy walked up, looking at me, asking who I was. She said, "This man is your daddy, your father."

The boy said, "Hi, are you really my daddy?"

My son's mother, at that point, was mad as hell, coming to see for herself.

The boys had to go in for school. My baby mama and I agreed to visit them at their house and spend time with the boy. Not once did she say anything about a husband or boyfriend. One day, I pulled up, waiting for the boy to come out. Instead, a dude came out tripping, saying crazy shit that I wanted his bitch, all types of shit. So we got into it. My arm went through a picture glass on their front door. The fight stopped. Blood from my arm was everywhere. I took off my T-shirt, tightly holding my arm, slowly falling out. They put me into my car, and taking me to the hospital. I woke up three weeks later with thirty-six stitches. I was actually dead on arrival, on May 6, 1998, at 3:32 p.m. The only thing left to say about that was God was on my side. The question is, why me? My baby mama and son said that they cried and prayed for my return almost every night.

Coming home, I met a man and his family who had just bought the house next door. He even fixed up the house nicely. Talking to him, he said that he owned his own company rehabbing houses and needed someone to work with him whom he could trust to run his crew when he left. The job paid $20 an hour. I said yes, changing my life around for the last time. It was worth it. Now my family was proud of me. I stopped drinking everything and stopped running the streets once again. But still, not seeing my family, my mother, or sisters. Shit like this hurts, not being wanted or loved by your own. But it made me stronger. My family and I were happy, doing good things, going out to movies and dinner. We even went out fishing.

The old man and I worked hard, twelve hours a day, like father and son. Even his wife treated me like her own son. The reason was their son had gotten killed back in the early '90s. We stayed family and neighbors for eight years strong. One day, while I came in from work, the old boy was at home sick. The police and ambulance were at his house. I could feel that he was gone in my heart. Getting in the house, his wife hugged me so tight with tears running down her face, saying that he had died in his sleep around 2:00 p.m. The only person who loved me and treated me like his own was gone.

After his funeral, his wife sat me down, explaining how much he loved me and wanted me to keep the business going. I was the boss of the crew, the head overseer, and she was the payee. After a while, my baby mama wanted out of our relationship because she was seeing another younger dude who was in his twenties, all this while I was at work. What's crazy as hell was that the old boy's wife wanted me anyway. At that time, I moved in to get on my feet. I let the old girl have everything—the cars, TVs, and radio.

After everything went down, my son told me that his real father was coming home from prison and that his father was my cousin. I thought back to the day when my cousin and I had a threesome with her in East Cleveland. I was shocked. Now my boss's wife let me move in, paying extra well for sex and work. Everything was laidback; the food and her sexy old self made this relationship last for two years. Then she died.

In the midst of it all, she was selling out the business under my nose. The only things I walked away with were $25,000, the tools, and two trucks. Moving from house to house, going through women was killing me. I had to move into a hotel until I found somewhere to rent on my own. Starting over again at thirty-four was nuts. They said she died of natural causes.

Sitting in my room, drinking some beer, I thought about everything that had happened in my life. It was wild and crazy as hell. The next morning, I went up Kinsman Road to the CMHA building to reapply for their apartments. Just by luck, an old friend of my mother was the head boss. She sent me to some apartments on Hough named Springbrook. The apartment was clean and quiet, so I signed the lease. I had to sell one of the trucks. I sold it to a man in the building for $3,500. Now I had $28,000 in my pocket to start over with. People in the hood knew me and were watching me closely. I went to a place called Furniture Warehouse, spending $11,000 on all new stuff, TVs, and a stereo system for $5,000. I needed some clothes and shoes for $3,500, watches, earrings, and diamond bracelets for another $3,500. That came up to a good $23,000 and some change, which was good.

Now I could go to the outpatient rehab at Recovery Resources on Twenty-Fifth and Detroit. This drinking and sometimes smoking that shit was killing me. I got my ass up there, signing in. The group was mixed and going well for the first day. I thought about AA meetings everywhere in Cleveland that I could go to. The women staff and clients were eyeing me down. A few days into coming to the group, I started talking to a lady. She wanted help because she was homeless and wanted out of street life.

She had a body and good looks, plus I needed some company at my apartment. She was a good cook, putting weight on me quickly. Not knowing that she wanted her cake and to eat it too, I went to sleep one day, waking up to see a nut on my living room floor. Lies were told about the nut I put out. She came with the police, saying that we had just had a baby and she paid me to live there with money and sex.

She even had some niggas playing games on my phone, so I got my St. Clair girl to get on her ass. They beat the shit out of her, putting her out of my house. Still, she wanted in. We both still went to the group, pretending like we were happy as hell. A few months went by, and we were done with the group. Then out of nowhere, her daughter wanted to come and move in with us. I paid her way. I traded in my truck for a new car. I still had a few dollars in the bank and had just gotten my SSI back pay of $19,000. I stayed looking good, her too, and her daughter. After that, her son came out of nowhere and needed somewhere to lay his head. But CMHA wasn't having that shit. They really wanted to put me out, so I moved out before anything could happen, losing it for life.

We rode around looking on the west side, a place I had never been but where they were from. At the same time, we both stayed sober and went to our AA meetings. Riding down a street called Archwood, a house downstairs was for rent. I paid the rent, $1,300 upfront, $775 a month. It was worth it because everyone had their own room, two doors for in and out, a living room, and a dining room, with a backyard for my car to park. But the same thing happened: everyone was working beside her. She started fucking a dude two houses down. The street was talking hard about her, calling her nasty and wondering why I was still with her. I married her after the first six months.

Shit was crazy because they called me Dad when they needed and wanted something. Knowing they never liked me, and still, to this day, after seven and a half years, they don't like me. We fought a few times, and I went to jail twelve times for domestic violence. That's crazy, and we don't have any kids together. Things got so bad, I had to put her kids out of my house. Her son was lying about work, her daughter was bringing dudes around my house, fucking and sucking around the garage, eating up everything, and not cleaning after themselves. I moved from there because the landlord was a good liar about fixing things.

I moved to the east side again, to St. Clair, Sixty-First, and Lausche. The house looked messed up, but I had people fix it up for me on the low, and I helped with the work. The rent was only $350, so why not? I knew just enough people who smoked weed all day, every day. I got myself two pounds and never looked back. I had a pit bull and two 9 mms that shot seventeen times per clip. Her daughter and her new dude moved downstairs, and my play cousins lived a block away. They were from upper St. Clair, where I was from, so we were all eating, doing big boy shit.

I was grossing $1,000 every day and found out that her oldest son lived just three streets away. He had kids that came over and played. The playground was across the street. We had cookouts almost every weekend. Drinking came back into our life, but now when she got drunk, fights started, and the police took me to jail. My weed would go missing, and most of my money. She was giving my stuff away and buying friends from her kids and neighbors. Rumors even said she was fucking dudes in the hood.

She did not know that her daughter never liked her either; everything to her was a game of having me and her mother. My wife had serious issues with her past. She was abused, and her kids' father in the past would beat her badly and take her money and put her on the block, selling ass. That was her life until she met me. This is why I stayed with her, to protect her and show her real love, breaking my back to keep us happy.

One day, while riding around selling weed and drinking, she got drunk as hell; she thought I was the kids' father who wanted to kill her. She jumped out of the car, screaming, "Help me. He's trying to kill me!" I was just around the corner, drinking and driving with no license, with a gun and a pound of weed under the seat. With no choice, I went home, telling her daughter and her dude. They rode around looking for her, only not to be found or seen. We called the police and reported her missing. Two weeks went by. Our fights continued. Her daughter recalled the police, saying that I had killed her and put her somewhere in an empty house. The police came, twenty deep, with a search warrant, taking my car and me to jail.

Shit was crazy. Afraid now that the other murders might show up, they were just about to read me my rights and charge me for murder without a body due to the twelve DVs I had with her. The phone rang; it was a detective from the Kinsman area saying that he had her in his car and was bringing her there. Her story was that she was walking home drunk when a black car pulled up to her, asking if she needed a ride. She asked them if they knew me and if they would bring her home. She passed out, waking up naked, and they were running a five-man train on her somewhere on Union and 124th Street. That's why the police found her over that way.

While she was gone and I was in jail, her kids took everything—the TVs, my stereo, my watches, rings, clothes, and diamonds. The house was left wide open. I still let her back in. The reasons I put up with their shit were unclear. Some of it was still feeling sorry for her, and maybe I was in love with her. Everyone thought they had found everything, but I buried a pound of weed, my gun, and $15,000 on the basement floor in cement.

Back to hustling, the police messed up my car badly. Her daughter wanted it so bad, I let her have the damn thing. Everything else they sold. I hustled enough to move, but in the midst of getting back on my feet, a man and his girl I knew down the street were robbed and killed in broad daylight. Across the street was a high school; they were getting out, seeing the bodies on the ground. A lot of people were saying they were looking for me; that was supposed to be me. They got the right color house but the wrong house. I got out of the game and moved to Forty-Third Street off St. Clair.

While everything was going wrong for me, my family reached out to let me know that my mother had passed from cancer. I took my last $5,000 to help with her house and whatever else was needed, but I never went back there for anything because they were still on that bullshit about my brother. Even today, we are not talking. I went back to East Cleveland and got a job doing custodial work in a group home that paid under the table. I still had four ounces of weed left. I was good. Her kids were never heard from again for a great while. We had our life back. She stopped doing crazy shit.

Some people had moved across the hall—a house full of nothing but hoes. They were tripping about me being a young, sexy Black man and my wife being White. Those hoes were drunks and weed heads, dressing like strippers up and down the street. The house smelled like shit.

Keeping myself and my wife from letting their trip become our trip, just as long as they didn't put their hands on her, we were good. But for real, breaking her down, she started tripping hard, thinking that I was going over to their house and not going to work. Her sons started coming around again, needing a place to stay, pulling me away from my own house. All hands needed something all the time, pushing my back against the wall with stress. She even had them thinking that I was going over there. She and I started drinking again, and she called the police, and I went to jail for DV. She had everyone thinking that I was jumping on her. Sometimes I was, but only after she kept pulling knives on me, trying to cut me. Crazy as shit.

So I started hanging out on a new block after work. Sometimes I even stopped coming home. I wanted out. She picked up and left again, this time having me really paying the bills. Her kids and she were gone, not knowing shit. This lasted for about six months when I had to move again.

I moved to a street in the hood, a street named Bayliss. I did not know anyone or anything about this street; this street was empty, with just one wild family living there. The hood hung out there where everything and anything went on—shooting dice, murders, rapes. All types of guns were shot almost every night. This is where my life changed again. My name went from Snoop to Chicken Wayne, and now it was Carwash.

Watching all these young thugs hanging out, I hung out on my porch, drinking my beer, trying to feel out my surroundings, not knowing they had burned a man alive next door to my house right before I moved there, and a girl down the street in a field was beaten to death and burned as well. This street was off the chain. Drug sales were there, so the only hustle that could keep me alive was washing cars at a low price—$7 a car. It started going hard until other car washes started hating on me. Shit, I had the hood on lock with that, making $300 a day or better.

But they were still trying to find me, setting me up, leaving cars for hours with guns, large amounts of money, and ounces of drugs in them. One guy played me like I was a snitch, thinking I just came out of the blue and was an old dude with strong polish about myself. They sometimes got drunk and high, messing with me hard like they wanted to kill me and see where I came from. I never told them shit about that. I had to get in the clique as Uncle Carwash. Being Uncle Carwash came with respect, and I had to put in more work.

We rode around. I was like the hitman because I never talked. I just kept my hand on the gun, ready to kill at will, any day or night. These young dudes wanted to be gangsters and drug dealers. I had to keep them alive. Their grandmother lived right next door to me.

Young and old women were always at my door, wanting to chill and spend the night with me. My wife, once again, was never around. But within that year of living on Bayliss, man, there were a lot of drug deals, gunfights, and dice games. Most of the time, we hung out at Chillie's, a store on Sixty-First or Norwood, for drink-outs and more dice games. Just the hood thing. Everybody came to kick it. The vice raided us. Some went to jail; everybody jumped over fences. After a few of them came home from jail, the truth was told. The police were looking for two bank robbers and three murderers. Everything in the hood was questioned.

Learning the reason the vice and the feds came down on us, we had shut down the hood hustle from the phone in codes. People getting robbed and shot. A few were killed, they say, by other hoods. It was a cover-up from the police. They were killing us off. Shit got crazy and wild as hell. Everyone moved off Bayliss. It became a ghost town. I was the last one to leave. My play cousins lived down Sixty-First off St. Clair, a different type of hustler. They hustled the same way but only to their own people from the west side.

They had an empty apartment they wanted $375 for, with no deposit. The only thing was that the lights and gas needed to be turned on. I moved in at the end of July. The light and gas company came out, saying there was a leak in the pipe, and the lights had to be replaced from the street poles to the house and the basement. It cost a lot of money, a little at a time. I understood. Besides, I ate and cooked downstairs at their house.

But now it was fall time, still no lights or gas. It was getting so cold, I had to sleep in my coat and street clothes to stay warm, and I had to take baths at their house as well. I felt a lot better being there with them than on Bayliss, even though I kept the AKs and most of the guns.

Shit started coming together once we bounced from the hood to the Westside. A few months went by, and not knowing anyone, even our relationship was going well, drinking and being sober. One day, being me, I had to get out and find some type of hustle. I was out trying to cut grass and rake leaves. An old lady a few houses down hit me back, saying $50 to cut her grass, which only took a few minutes. That got me thinking if she was paying for something that crazy, what else would she pay for?

My thinking was right. I showed her my dick, and she went crazy for it, paid me $100 just to touch it. I went and told my wife, money in hand, laughing. The next day, another $100 just for talking. My wife started to get mad about the old lady trying to take her man. So we got drunk as well. She called the police. I bounced back to the Eastside, always with a few dollars in my pocket. My people and I started kicking it hard until the next day, an all-nighter.

It was 6:30 a.m., and shit started ending on that block. So I went down to the next block, Sixty-First and Superior, where everything and everybody was. I walked in on some shit off the start, hitting a lick. My dude needed somebody to watch his back while he robbed a trap house. Shit went down. He came out, and we were walking the street with him, talking big boy shit. A small gray car pulled up slowly. Two guys jumped out. One shot at me, hitting me in the leg. I started running and bleeding. My dude got a gun straight to his head. I was up the street, going inside an empty old house. I heard two shots from that way. It was my nigga. They killed him. They got back in their car.

Still to this day, I never said shit or knew shit. My leg had a flesh wound. My wife was tripping harder, wanting me to come home, but the police were riding hard, looking for me. Also, her so-called family was coming over and calling, seeing if I made it home yet so they could jump me. All this bullshit.

I had been in the hood now for a week. Really, no one was talking about what had happened to my nigga because it's said you live by the gun, you die by the gun. That's real shit. So I went home to my wife to kiss and make up. Shit died down for a week, maybe. Then it started up again, and now I was in the county jail, biting my nails on two M3s and a rape and murder from 2008 in East Cleveland. The detectives' questioning fucked her head up, making her think I did that shit. But the detectives promised that in seven weeks if the DNA came back showing I had anything to do with it, I would be charged with the murder and rape. My brain was blown.

After a week in jail, we had just moved into a new house with different police speaking of them bitches. Their station was right down the street, and their back was my front door. Yeah, that type of shit. And my wife was a caller too. Wow.

She had problems, but who doesn't? That's my ride-or-die, my rib. That's why I married her. We did wrong to each other. Court time was coming up in the morning, on November 19, 2019. There was no word about my shit, which must be good on my half, right? I couldn't reach the old bitch or my wife's phones. They weren't taking calls. The old lady was eating the shit out of some pussy now and paying. Who would I choose, right? Seven years with my wife were all as crazy as wars, but she was still standing strong. The old hoe, a few months and more, faced damn problems than a nigga could take, for real. But seriously, she paid, which was no money, you feel me.

Back to the hood. I lived there for about a year, and I will promise you that there have been over fifteen murders on hand count that I could remember. Now I was out of jail. I had to go back to the east to the doctor just to see my young dude's name on a building freshly painted with "RIP." I had to go in tripping. We both were because I had just met him like two months back downtown with me coming from the Justice Center. I was damn near fifty years old, faking and acting like this was still my life, right? This is why she took my bitch ass out of the hood. The hustle stayed in me, old or young. I even turned my life around by being a working man, twelve hours a day, and broke my foot trying to turn my life around to be a better man for my wife.

But thinking a few years back, being in the hood, drinking, smoking, staying on the block all night long, seeing shit that went past us, we watched one time a car chase. Four dudes jumped out. The other car was shooting at them, killing all four one by one, all on Superior. Right after that, a police chase ended deadly in front of Mr. C's store on Superior. Then that one time, we were all in the back of the gas station. We heard gunshots. We came around to see what was up. The owner shot a robber.

On the other blocks, we were welcome, but I started my own block in the hood. It was the gas station. The right way to make money was by pumping gas and cleaning windows. I kept an Old English 24 in my hand. All that was when me and my wife had gotten into it. Fifty-Fifth and Superior was my second home.

But what's really fucked up is when I lived on Bayliss, right next door to me, right before I moved there, a man was robbed and killed inside his truck, burned alive. I met an Indian girl that I let stay with me, shorty, and right across from the gas station; her body was found, and her head was in a trash bag in the same field. She had been missing for about two weeks before anyone cared about her. The next day, I pumped a man's gas, and down the same street where she was found, he was found with two gunshots to his head. A bad drug deal went bad. But all this to say, this is why my wife took me out of the hood.

Now in the new hood, Memphis, meeting a few hood niggas made me feel at home. But my one dude grew on me like a brother as time went on. But in the back of my head, he kept telling me that he didn't feel safe living there with his sister and dude. Well, just a few days ago, he got killed, shot in the back of his head in his bed while asleep. Her dude killed him over nothing. A good dude was gone. My play daughter was on the news after his death. She got killed, and shot in the back.

A lot of people were saying it was *jealousy* from a girl that just got made in that new gang shit, the hardened felon. But speaking of them, the jails were full of them, the people who ran it too. They were young in that street shit. Cleveland was nothing but that one big street gang. Believing this was really crazy as hell. My second time being locked back up, they were still in there, the same ones, the young kids.

Hell, I was a folk. Back in my days, there were Vice Lords, Crips, Bloods, and us Folks, and some mean street gangsters, but not just one set. Even old people were dealing like they were young too. The overturn here was crazy, and the girls, the women, were loving it more. All jailbird shit inside this Justice Center. The COs were mostly young girls with clan backgrounds working the system. All the dudes were too afraid or something. It was real crazy inside there.

The judges were working their hands like this on DV cases. They had their own police force to take your girl to a place like you were trying to kill them or something, and your bond on these cases was high as hell.

All this came from a judge killing his wife, a girl on the freeway killed and thrown out of the car, a girl's brother killing her over a car that wasn't even hers, and then on top of it all, a baby in a trash bag dead on Clark. Huh, shit was really crazy in Cleveland.

What was really crazy was that I was still sitting in a jail cell. I had just talked to my wife after court today. Shit went left field, all over my money that she just came and got. Remember that I was in there for her dumbass shit, her calling the police after midnight. Why do women do it? Call the motherfucking police. Yeah, women were crazy. They were in their own world. Couldn't live with them, and couldn't live without them. Join the club. Their game truly was sold and not told. But sitting in this jail cell, man, was becoming crazy. So many young lives were being taken. About 80 percent of them would get out and get killed, maybe in a year's time. Black or White, in the streets, there were three women or girls to one man. The girls were growing up to be gay, and the dudes were in the joint learning how to become gay. It's the world now. But me, I loved pussy. I had a wife and six grandkids that I could count. Three sons were doing life in Ohio prison systems.

All my kids had no father, even though I really wanted to and tried my hardest to be one. But the life I was living was too dangerous for their safety. Trust me, it hurt not to see or hear from them, but in the end, it was all for the best. I understand that now. From the gang life to the street life, it's a wonder why and how I'm still alive.

My nine lives ended a long time ago. It's my life with God; he kept me here.

But I do have a granddaughter. She was four, and that girl is my world. She kept me alive. I smiled just thinking about her. She's hard-headed and never gives up. Truth be told, she's my wife's grandbaby, but to that little one, I could never do any wrong.

On May 6, 2019, I was walking toward the CUS Corner Store to get some beer. I remember seeing a man walking close to me. I turned to go inside the door and heard three gunshots. The shots hit me in the leg, arm, and chest. I lay face up, looking at the sky, hearing talking and screaming, "Get him some help!"

A duty nurse was putting her hands on my chest wound, saying, "It will be okay. Hold on. Help is coming." I could hear my wife by my side, crying her heart out. I was losing blood, and my body was getting colder. The police were there.

Three months later, after being in a coma, my wife was still by my side, happy tears falling. She and the doctor said it would be hard to walk again. I was still in jail, learning how we moved out of the hood only to get shot. Wow. But later, from hearing stories, the word was it was a hit from 1983, me stealing someone's car. The same old man who blew up my house, trying to kill me and my family, missed us by a few minutes. I remember watching the car ride past me, pointing a gun at me. We heard a loud boom and saw fire in the street, our couch across the street smoking. At the age of twelve, my life was like that, doing big boy things.

Mom was tripping and crying. My baby sister who was around three years old was in a walker. I got us back together that same night. We spent the night over at her friend's house. I went to Fifty-Fifth and Woodland, hitting up that game room and corner store, getting around $6,000. Mom found a single house on Sixty-Sixth and Beauer. I went back to jail, doing the rest of my ten years. The hood told an old lady who saw me going in and out of the game room. The old man was later found running down the street, burning alive. Not my call, just the way it was in Cleveland. Someone was always doing something, and someone always remembered things.

Five years went by quickly. Coming home at eighteen and a half in June 1988, the summer was going. Wade Park, Eighty-Sixth Street, and Ansel Road were my new hood, turning it out with gunplay. But the story was already told at the beginning of the book. Just when I started thinking that shit would get better, it turned for the worst.

My stepson had a good job making $17.50 an hour at a factory, working twelve hours a day, five days a week. Some dudes on the block were watching him come in and out with his family and new stuff. They blacked out in black masks and clothes, kicking the door in, taking his TVs, games, computers, and a few hundred dollars, shooting him twice in the chest. It hit me hard. I got my family six deep. Folks called, hitting their block, finding and painting shit up, out of sight, out of mind. My stepson was still fighting for his life in Metro. My oldest child was taking it hard, and I too, because I accepted him like my own son.

Fixing up the house, my wife and I, along with another son, were trying hard to get money. One of us came up with a plan, hitting a house for copper pipes. We had been watching the house. It was dark, and we walked in with flashlights. Inside, we saw a new refrigerator, a new stove, and a microwave. The house was clean. Looking inside the fridge, there was a twelve-pack of Miller High Life, old as hell. We took a drink—it was too old to drink. We left and planned to come back at daybreak, which we did, only to find an old-ass couch eaten up by rats and newspaper. A dresser with rat-eaten clothes was inside. In the bedroom, there was a bed with a metal box frame and a moving truck blanket wrapped around it, looking like a body. We unwrapped it, and bones appeared, looking like a lady. We left and went home, telling my wife our story.

We got a truck just to take the new stuff, and then she called the police for a welfare check. They came and found the body. The newspeople were there, and everybody was watching, tripping on the find. We stood in the crowd. The next day, her son came to see what had happened. He asked if anyone wanted to make a few dollars cleaning out that house. We said yes. My stepson was on his way home, so we put on plastic suits and picked up the bed and couch, taking them and thrashing them out on the street. We slammed them on the ground. Rats ran out everywhere, people scattered, and even the newspeople.

The newspeople jumped back inside their truck and took off. It looked like at least fifty rats. That crazy day was over. Now we had enough money, so when my son and his brother came home, he could relax.

The next day, he came home. The first thing he wanted was some weed and an Old E, and to sit and kick it with us—a family thing. The hood was happy; it was back to normal. No police, guys back on the block doing their thing—it was peaceful.

A week went by. My second son and I were walking to the store on the corner right up our street. Cars were riding by. I had 9 mm on my hip, left side. I was walking in the middle. A small gray four-door car drove by, looking hard at us. I pulled and cocked my 9 mm. My son did too. We got to the store and went in. After standing for a few minutes, watching our backs, the car was gone. So we bought a bag of beer, some milds, and Newport.

We saw the car inside the parking lot, but the dudes were not inside the car. A lady who knew us walked in.

She said, "Watch out. They are out there asking questions about you with guns."

So we were ready to die if we had to. The store owner got his gun and cocked it too. We all came out with guns pulled. We started shooting. The driver got hit in the head. The other dude started shooting and running down the street toward my house. My guys heard the shooting, looked, and started shooting at the dude.

Now we had him in the middle of the street. People were running for cover. His gun ran out of bullets. No one on my side was hurt. Thank you, Jesus, for that. He got shot once in the shoulder. We took him across the street into an empty building, beating him with the gun handle, asking him why and who sent him to us. He gave in and started saying it was the old man who started this shit from the beginning. It was his brother. We had killed the old man a few months back.

We were all in disbelief about this old-ass family and their heart. Shit was not going to stop—blood for blood. We were thinking of letting him go, so we did, after a week of torture. After that, we started getting short. A few went missing, a few got beaten and kidnapped. My son and I went hard early in the morning, setting his shit on fire, shooting everything that moved—cat, dog, rat. We wanted it dead. We killed the old-ass mommy, the daddy, their other brother, him, and one son.

Happy now. Life could go back to normal. Even their neighbors were happy they were dead. That's bad, huh? But now the block was hot as hell. I mean, the FBI, local police, and the sheriffs were riding hard, questioning everyone who lived in the 44105 area code. All GDs were in hiding, gangsters hiding. After three weeks, shit started going back to normal. The case went to cold case profiles. Still, to this day, there's a reward of $100,000.

About six months had gone by. Everybody was doing their thing, and no one ever spoke of that shooting anymore. We thought it was completely over. One of the old man's sons, who was in prison in Kentucky, came to Cleveland searching for answers about his family. It was like running from the ghosts that you killed, with no face. Believe this: he even stood next to me in the store. I never knew who he was until a crackhead told me it was the old man's son. I asked if he was really sure, and the store owner said the same thing. I was like, "Damn, now I have to watch him and see what's up with him too."

He got high on crack, so we had him on lock. I got older, my sons had kids, and we moved out of the hood. Hell, even the hood turned over. My wife started getting sick a little at a time. I was walking with a cane, my feet messed up with steel in them. We got away from the East to the West, but we kept all eyes on that dude and never spoke of the killing again. It blew over, and everything was everything.

Wifey was cool about it. Everybody came out okay. Me, just this small stuff in court. It's cool, trust me, as long as there's no murder on file. But July 13, 2018, was the year my dude who taught me the game got himself killed in a bar on Superior. Some past tense came back to get him. They sent a known crackhead to see if he was in there, and if he was, to tell him someone was outside messing with his truck. That worked. He came out tripping with his gun in his hand. The setup was on the side of the building. They sprayed him with sixty-two shots, killing him like a dog. Thirty-five years old, gone.

My other G was coming out of the store when his car blew up. I was in and out of jail. Like now, years after that killing, is it payback? At my dude's funeral, he was in the casket looking good. Men in black came in, shooting up his casket and then kicking it over. The family ran out crying and in fear. No one saw anything or heard anything after that. His body went to Lakeview. My family members were all in there—the older ones, the young ones in Riverside, speaking and graveyards.

I worked at Lakeview graveyard for a while, trying to change my life and find my family's old graves. There's a duck pond there. In 2002, my daughter's cousin was found shot in the head in that pond. I saw the body but never met him before. My wife says that when you do the crime, you have to do the time, or you live by the gun, you die by the gun. She knew his baby mama. She lost her mind after that happened. I stopped working there too. He was lying in a pond of his own blood. The news hit it for a week.

My wife and I just stayed in the house, tripping on everything that life brought—the good and the bad. We were still alive and trying to stay away from people, places, and things. It didn't last long. My old girl that I was messing with for money; now her son was looking for me to kill me again. She told him that I was taking her money and beating her. Drama, right? I got with him on some other shit. I took a video of his mother, sucking me and my wife, and showed him where I was hitting, letting him see how much she enjoyed my company. The problem lifted out the door with him. Now things should be drama-free—me and my wife and against the world. We moved out of the hood, but the hood was still in me. That's some stuff.

Speaking of the hood, I remember when every gas station, corner store, and most homeowners—the "Arabs"—came to Ohio, to Cleveland with briefcases full of money. Black people started selling their souls, just in that order: store, home, and gas stations. Now every home was abandoned. The corner stores were mostly shut down. On each street, there were over forty houses. Now maybe none were still acceptable to live in. Nothing was hardly Black-owned. On every street corner, there are crowds of Black men and women selling drugs or using them. Everyone wants to become thugs.

The police set up to take everyone to jail for everything—a week for an open beer, seriously. Mostly everything that's going on, even the free food centers is closing. No jobs for people with criminal records. The system is designed to lock you up for walking across a street. That's prison time—six months for a $5 bag of weed. If your girlfriend just says that you did something to her, that's at least four months in the county jail. If you steal a bag of chips or gum from a store, that's six months in prison. The system is for failures, especially for Black people.

Our people are growing up with no fathers who care or want to be real men, showing them how to become men. And young girls are growing up with their mothers like that's something good to do. Neither one knows how to cook, go to work, or keep a house. When I was growing up, most families didn't have men in their lives, but the mother was both father and mother. The neighbor saw you do something wrong; they could get that ass. Your mother could get that ass, with anything and anywhere. We grew up learning how to respect ourselves and others, and how to become men. It was a choice of how you wanted to be, trust that.

But back to the story. My son was back to normal from his wounds. The hood was back together. The thing was, other hoods were coming down, jumping guys and pocket-checking. I was on the run with two F4 warrants here in Cleveland. That's like thirty years, really for nothing. The other shit was still cold cases. That's love there. Man, I was fifty years old now, and once again, my wife was a crazy, police-calling ass, and she was sick. My hands were full with her stuff.

And my granddaughters, who were four and six, acted like they were my mommy and I was the grandpa and daddy. And I loved them the same way. Those kids made me smile, my wife too. She acted like them, watching cartoons all the time like she was a kid.

I was sitting on my couch, writing this book. Out of the corner of my eye, I saw a black car pull up, and two tall white men jumping out. Seeing that gold badge, I was tripping. They could come into the house searching. I ran upstairs. There was a small hole in the wall that you couldn't see. I could hear the footsteps coming up the stairs.

The voices were getting really heavy. Doors were opening. My wife kept saying, "He's not here. He moved away a month ago," due to our relationship.

The police were getting smart with her, saying, "Bitch, shut up. We know he's here." The closet door opened. I could see the flashlight hitting the hidden door. They were moving my clothes around. Then it got really quiet. They were still standing there as if they could see my door or hear me move.

Five minutes went by. My wife said, "Babe, they're gone. Come out." Happy as hell that they were gone, we got drunk that day. After that, no more police came to the house, but I was still on the run. They even posted up in an unmarked car at the corner, watching me go in and out. But I was using the private door they used.

One day they played me good. They were on my street on another call or whatever, so I walked right past them going to the store. I saw their car outside writing, so I did what I always do, going out the other door. As I opened the door, the handcuffs went on my wrist. Two cars were full of these hating-ass bitches. I was in the back seat, riding bitch my damn self, going to the county jail downtown Justice Center. It took hours just for them to take me up to the eleventh floor. B6 was my cell. My court date started on December 3, 2019. Man, this was like my fourth time in this bitch. I was looking at two years max for two grams, $500, and an empty-ass gun that was in my back pocket. I saw these motherfuckers I hadn't seen in a long time, all types of folks, and just hood people from over Cleveland. They serve three hot meals a day, two to a cell. A month in this bitch, then just eighteen months down in Lorain. 2021 was my out date.

My wife was my heart, my ride or die. She was cool. Her pockets were full. I made that happen hustling, but my kind of hustling, fucking with that crack, I saw a lot of people selling their daughters to dope boys. Daughters and mothers did threesomes and stayed in empty-ass houses just to keep their money for crack. From selling that shit, the fame got to my head, buying everything I needed for my house, clothes, and pussy from the finest women in the hood at that time.

Man, jail is the worst place. I had a spot in my stomach that was really fucked up since birth. I couldn't go like regular people. I had to take medicine to go, and also get put to sleep so they could pump out my stomach from polyps. That problem had come back. My stomach was bleeding due to internal and external hemorrhoids, which were stopping everything. Even when I farted, it hurt. I was a man with no fear or tears, but being in here sick was fucked up. My dude from Seventy-Ninth died in here from a headache. In two months, nine people had died from drug reactions or something. It was really crazy like that in here. But with no money in your pocket, you were forced to eat this nasty-ass shit. And they gave you a kid tray of that shit. Strong-minded men made it, right? I was really trying to chill and stay out of the way.

Yeah, looking outside my window at my door, I could see that three of my old school friends had just come. One was right next door to me. The other came into my cell, tripping on this nasty-ass food and the women COs that worked in here. We talked about what was going on on the outside. There were a lot of empty houses and more young kids dying. Man, it was like three kids a week, damn near shooting each other for small stuff or robbing for crack money. And the girls in those tight-ass leggings, the rapist niggas didn't rape the women looking like that in leggings, showing the world. They raped the women that wore clothes on their asses.

But yeah, we hit on talking about a little girl up the way. She was killed, fucked up. Her mother owed money for crack. The Jamaicans raped and cut that little girl up into pieces all over the Kinsman area. The dogs were eating her legs and arms when they found parts of her. Her head was found inside an empty dump truck in a tall-ass field of grass. Later, her legs were found in a field down the way. Her stomach was burned behind their house two streets away in burning leaves. That shit hit home. Everyone had kids, and no arrest was ever made. Ooh, that house fire on Superior Eighty-Fourth, four kids and the mother all dead inside over a jealous-ass nigga, and it was the wrong house that he had set on fire. Crazy as shit.

Talking the old shit, these two old-ass niggas just told me the reason they were in here. They stole a car and went to Fifty-fifth and Superior, to the Key Bank, and robbed it, getting away with $10,000. They went down the next two streets and jumped out. They saw a trick bitch, went to her and her friend, smoking crack for about a week in hiding. But they went broke smoking crack, turned around, and robbed the crack dealer for something nice. They said they put the drug dealer in the trunk and the two tricks took them uptown Miles somewhere into a graveyard and left them there.

Okay, this shit was at nighttime, at around 12:30 a.m. They were high as hell. They walked right into the police who were waiting on them with guns out. They got some crack, a few dollars from a dude, and the guns. Wow, that's crazy. These niggas were in their fifties. We started talking about the time we all first met at the strip club on Wade Park.

I had just come home after doing ten years. I was sitting at the bar drinking. They were shooting pool. A stripper was dancing on the corner. One had an ice tray, putting it in her pussy. The one in front of me was smoking a Newport with her shit. Now I was half drunk, tripping on what I was seeing. I saw something small fall into my drink. I threw up all on the stripper. They put me out of the bar. At the same time, they wanted to kill me. That's when my niggas jumped the bouncers. After that, we got cool. All of this talking we had been doing, and it was breakfast time. The COs were letting us out of our cells. We looked next door to get our dude. His ass was in there fucking that boy. He looked back, saying that twenty years was a long, lonely time, and he was starting right now. The boy said, "Jay, my handle, that ass is yours, baby." We were really tripping. Should we pull him out and kick his ass or just let it be?

Anyway, the COs were coming. It was like they smelled the peanut butter in the air. The boy got up and pulled his clothes up, smelling laughter all the way to "Coow." That's how it was. But look, this wasn't prison yet. Down there, you would see niggas fucking cows, pigs, and sheep. And this shit got crazier by the damn minute.

The CO who just let us to "Coow" was looking at us really strong. We were like, "What the fuck," thinking that we would have to kick his ass. Coming back, he started talking and asking really strong-ass questions about what hood we were from, did we knew people. He went on talking, and we were playing the game right along with him, seeing what was up with him. We were like, "Yeah, Wade Park. We lived there back in the day." This nigga asked us if we knew the dude whom we had robbed for two keys and $200,000. It was like he knew that we were the ones who did it to his cousin. This nigga was one of the ones who could kill inmates with his crew and get away with it. And my two niggas were about to ride out. Damn, it was all bad.

A few days went by and turned into a month. That day came. They rode out. Now it was me and the CO. At this time, he kept tripping, asking more and more questions. One day he came and took me with his crew to an empty floor. They jumped me, asking questions. No correct answer. They let me go, but my insides were fucked up. What could I do alone? So I made myself a knife out of a toothbrush.

Now believe this: the CO assigned me to work detail on every dorm on the eleventh floor, and he had been hiring inmates to paint me. Two have tried. I won and went to the hole, only to get beat more by his CO crew, half-ass giving me food. The water was brown with no kind of light. Roaches and rats were around. After a week, I got the hole for a few days. I felt free, I guess, to heal, but during that waiting period, it was my ride to Lorain, where even my niggas were at.

Getting off the Blue Bird, I looked so bad the white shirts asked, "What the hell happened to you?" I said I fell. My niggas were happy that I was alive and that payback would come painfully. That's what we lived for, and the young dudes who jumped me down there? Guess what? They had to come through us.

Wifey was happy that I was gone from downtown, but the drama was still awake because the young niggas were coming next week, and there would be a lot of shit. But right then, we were getting our game plan together and getting the COs in our right pocket. It's old school and new school. The COs saw how I looked when I came in, so we all had been working out, watching our *surroundings*, and listening to what was being said. Nothing was spoken, and no one was acting crazy, but my crew made knives and the old-school way of putting phone books around our sides.

We went to different dorms because the new ride-ins had just come. Two of those niggas just got off the bus, the third one somewhere else. So now it was time to work. Receiving dept. was the starting point. We acted like we wanted to clean and pass out water and food. We knew them; they knew me but not my dudes. We acted like we weren't together. Anyway, the COs gave us the sign to take off on them. The COs had them in a back room off in the cut. So we went into the room without a word and started working. Blood was everywhere. One was on the floor screaming for help, the other one fighting back but no win. The COs had to push the man-down button. We went to the hole, but at the same time, it was funny as hell that some old niggas *whooped* on some young niggas. When their niggas went in, this was some big shit.

Now there was Tone in the eighth house; I was in the five house, and Ant's crazy-ass in the third house. Their niggas were all in the seven houses. Tone was the one who was fucking those boys. They caught wind of it and set him up in the gym room bathroom, getting it in with some young-ass White boy afraid for his life. They used him, but yeah, they caught my nigga Tone with locks, in the sock, and bars of soap. They blacked his eyes, broke three of his ribs, and his arm in two places. Prison hospital for a week or two.

Ant was crazy. He just walked into their *coow* line, *busting* them niggas in their faces and going out. Now the *hole* shoot for two weeks. Now it was all on me, but I was the one who started the whole thing with the robbery. But I still had my homemade knife and my phone books. Knowing and seeing what I knew and watching my back, it was on. Now they have the police on their side. More money, more niggas.

Shit went slow for a while. Tone was gone. Ant was gone. I was walking around with my eyes on the back of my head. Voices I could hear from other dorms, people who weren't involved talking and seeing for me. That's the difference.

I stood two steps before them. They set me up to go walking on the track, and they were going to try to stick me and leave me for dead. Ant and Tone weren't around. I couldn't send any messages, so I had no choice. I went through with their plan. I walked with my phone books on my sides. Believe it, they sent a nobody to try the attempt.

The bus ride out for Mansfield was about to ride. Ant just got packed up. That's fucked up. Tone was still in the prison hospital. He was doing better. Wifey just had written. She was doing okay. The family was too. They just moved and bought a new house. It needed some work, straight out of the way. Far west. River Rock? No, Rocky River. It was a four-bedroom, two-bathroom, living and dining room, front and back porches, and a two-car garage for $83,593. That's good shit. My daughter was there with her. It was so good to hear from the other side of the fence. It's crazy, but her eyes were not that good, she kept saying.

At this time, the white shirts were on our ass. They were asking questions about these fights and murder attempts, so the prison warden *separated* us by night, riding me and Tone out to Mansfield. Now it was all three of us back together. The young niggas were left behind, which we all had thought. We had just enough time to wash our faces and brush our teeth before seeing those niggas get off the bus the next damn day. Wow. But this time there wasn't any drama with these dudes for the first six months.

The CO from Cleveland had gotten killed, shot in the head in his driveway with his work clothes on, going or coming from work at 8:30 a.m. It's funny in the hood that way, but *quietly* the beef went on. We had some old gangsters, St. Clair love. The young niggas grouped up. The shit started back up again. They caught me in the bathroom, and *stomped* me out; there were about ten of them. This time the same day, Ant was in the kitchen at *coow*. Tone was now fucking boys; he got caught up in the hat and was stomped out and killed.

Man, it was me and Ant, but Ant was acting like he wanted the other dudes. Rode with Tone, so now they were gone. The shit was too deep to make peace. After two days of Tone's death, the state of

Ohio ordered Tone's body to be in the state blues and laid inside a cardboard box and put six feet deep on their land. The White guy that he was fucking hanged himself inside Lorain.

My time was getting short; out of eighteen months, it was like seven on the top. Ant's shit was just starting on his twenty years set. Our other old schools were working their way, and now the young niggas had made peace. Unbelievable, but they did. Getting word from the street through other people, people said that two more of our young niggas off the block just got killed. One got shot in the head in the middle of Superior, and the other one on a porch, shot in the leg and died the next week. Later, a drive-by: my young dude's mother and her sister were sitting and minding their own business, drinking some beer. They got shot and died, his mother once in the head, and her sister twice in the chest.

Just hearing that bad news touched me for the first time in a long time. I felt tears from my eyes. My young dude was like a son to me, hanging with my sons, trying to keep them out of the way of drama, a mama's boy talking to my family. They as well, and no one had seen or heard anything. Just a drive-by. The shooting was meant for them niggas down the street, two houses down, where they hang out, shooting dice, and drinking all night long, mostly all the time, drug deals too.

My family had been asking me to stay out of trouble and come home and stay. This time, I was about to start going to some classes. Church? Me, church? Yeah, I'm tripping, but to save my marriage, it's going down. I loved that crazy woman. Me coming home to do what? I'd been a thug my whole life, but I liked detailing cars. That would be my new outlook on life. But like they say, if you don't see someone you know still in the street, they're dead or in jail. They're in jail.

The bus ride-ins come to Mansfield, like every two weeks, or like on a special ride, like mine was. These niggas had been down here for some years and still had time on their plate. That's crazy. Yeah, niggas that you wouldn't think are killers, they are. It's 80 percent of the hood in here. Also, they heard about them young niggas with that beef shit. And they took it over with smiles. They also lived for drama. Now I could rest and come home.

I had been talking to white shirts. They said, "Stay out of trouble for two months, and we'll send you to the camp." They did, and I went, smiling some shit up. It felt like coming home again. There was nothing as far as the eye could see but animals—cows, pigs, and horses. My job was to feed them, clean up their stalls, and learn how to milk the cows. All was a learning experience.

I could remember this day as if it was yesterday: the cows walking and lying in the tall grass. The farm CO had walked up to me and asked, "Do you believe in God?"

I said, "Yes, I'm still alive. Fresh air does something to you." The CO had walked away and seemed far away in minutes. The clouds were turning dark, good rain clouds, and the cows slowly started going back into the barn.

After that, I began to notice a lot of different *behaviors* in the cows and me. I was tripping, no one but me and two other inmates, and the CO. The CO was in and out so much it was like we, the inmates, ran the farm. I felt different. I started wanting to talk to God, asking questions, praying out loud when I was alone, seeing things that were there from the beginning, and forgiving my *enemies*.

Calling my family, saying that I loved them and that I missed them. They asked if I was okay, what was going on. The answer was that God opened my eyes, ears, and heart.

It was almost time for my release. I even wrote to a nearby church for me to become a member. My mind was going; my life was completely changed. This was what I needed: God in my life. My family started following me to church, my wife by my side.

All was good until June 3, 2019. A friend of mine was killed, and burned alive in a house with his daughter, during a robbery. His hustle got them killed. He was a millionaire in the hood; it put me back into my past quickly, drinking and wilding out. But out of it all, God had my back, wrongs and rights.

Their bodies were inside the trunk of a car in East Cleveland. It took six weeks. Their *funeral* was at the biggest church in Cleveland. They were buried together, father and daughter. A horse-drawn carriage took them down the way to a private graveyard. They had *cost* six people and were charged for the murders. He was a good duck, a good father. He will be missed. The tears to this day burn my eyes from the *swosh* murders. Too many. Look who's talking—after the things and the life that I am living.

I had two weeks left. I don't know what to do. People and places would be different. I guess my wife won this fight. Smiles. A good woman is like a second mother in that way, huh? There were hardly any good times in my life. Yes, I and my wife wanted to do something different. So we went to Walmart to buy fishing rods and tackles and went fishing. Because it was my first time, I threw the fishing rod inside.

The water was mad. Oh, I was mad. My wife started laughing, her here. Out everyone was. After thinking about it, it was funny to me too. She kept on catching fish, two at a time. On the inside, it made me even madder, but we were having a great time and we were sober. Watching her smile sometimes made me happy. That is what I would like to do: live for once, turning my life over to God and following his footsteps, fresh home, looking good on my wife's arm, people saying hi, and they were glad that I was home. The west side even smelled different and looked different. But our hood is fucked up—empty houses, tall grass, trash everywhere. Rats and roaches in the *available* houses that people live in. People all on the corners, standing by the stores, fronts anywhere where there's money.

My wife and daughter and grandbaby took me to the Red Lobster to eat, enjoying life. My wife's phone rang. More bad news arrived. My good friend from prison had gotten killed, and burned alive in a cell. The warden asked us if we wanted his body home. My wife said yes; we were his only family. I kept my head up, trying not to cry. My grandbaby hugged me tight with her little self, saying, "Grandpa, I love you. Don't go back home." That's what she called home for me: prison. She was four years old, right? Wow!

After that bad news, we just rode around looking and talking. My wife was telling me that my daughter was doing great in college. I was so proud and touched because she was doing better than us both, me and her mother. My wife's niece, she's right along with my daughter. There were a lot to be grateful for. They were studying to become doctors.

The next day we sat in the sun after a good breakfast, holding hands. She mentioned a power wash; there was no mobile wash around. She showed me a small building for a chicken spot, which cost around $50,000. That was all we had in the world. She said, "Never be afraid of making money. The building is in a good location, and my car wash will bring in money and keep me busy and out of trouble." So we did the business. We took it to the hood and lived on the west side. Things went slow for a while, just keeping bills paid. God blessed us every day with something.

One day the weather broke for the best of our business. We made a killing in one day: $5,000. So I let my wife add more to her thing and get more help. I was so proud of her and my daughter and her niece, all from God's hand.

This was the first time I was hustling without a crime being done, seeing the police and not having to shoot, fight, or run. This shit felt good, also to sit back and watch my wife do her thing. The hood was trying to come together in its own way. Believe it, I even washed a few police cars and got a tip. I started washing the light company cars and trucks, the local cable company, houses, and storefronts coming out good sometimes even at the bars. My wife's sister wanted in, so she went mobile, and came up using my wife's business. In the first six months, we grossed about $30,000 together, which was good from doing good shit. Sometimes we even had the grandbaby selling Kool-Aid in front of the store, she and her cousin doing their thing at six years old. Wow, it was a family thing now.

My wife's family moved to Cleveland from down south, getting in with us, and we grew as one, now making $100,000 a year without any crime. The police hated it. They even tried to close us down a lot, but God was good. Not! Hell, the building was paid for, and the local police and feds couldn't do shit but watch. My wife saw six apartments upstairs that needed some light work done, like painting and a little plumbing for $500 a month; that was $3,000 extra. Why not? And her people would come to live; this would be perfect. As you see, she had the brains—don't tell her that. Her family came to

Cleveland. We let them stay out in the store. I took the time out and hired a few good dudes to fix up the building. Man, it looked really good.

She wanted the hardwood floor look with flat white paint and new kitchen cabinets and new tubs. We just redid that part and put up ceiling fans and new bathroom cabinets as well. Also a new in-and-out door, all this in every unit. Now she could easily get $500, which now she was older like people our age and better. In her very first year in business, the girl was getting it. There was an empty store across the street she wanted. The same thing, it was cheap to buy and fix up. There was a lot still inside. The last owner had *cost up* in them drugs with street niggas being *around* there. It was a good location plus this was our hood. You know she did it. She paid $50,000 for it and another $50,000 for everything else. The money now was coming in four ways.

My grandbaby had grown so much in learning the business, also the payroll. My wife was so *proud* of her. She just sat back, and my baby ran the stores most of the time with no mistakes. The drawer was correct. Her mother was full of joy as well. As a reward, we were all taking her to Disney World for a week. Should I say my wife, my daughter, and my baby—a girls' day out, I called it. But to me, it felt really good not to have to kill or rob no one, just live. Most of the time I was walking with God. Me, yeah, me. My family all went to church. Today I didn't have to watch over my shoulders, see the police come into my stores, and not trip.

Since the girls were gone, I wanted to remodel our first house. So I got my nephew, and we went to look at it. I was telling him some stories about that house. "This is the house your aunt shot at me when I was fighting a guy over her dog. It was the wrong dog. Just when I was killing him, choking him." But my nephew didn't know that our plans were to give him this house for his family and give him my second power wash truck. The house just needed a fresh paint job, the carpet pulled up, and some hardwood floors down, to upgrade the yard. It had been empty for ten years. That was my safe house. It cost us money, but in the end, we were at peace.

I and nephew just got started working hard on his house. My wife and the family were okay, enjoying themselves. I couldn't believe how everything was working out. "God, God, I am going to wait until we are all together before I let him know the good news." My sisters had just bought a house on the west Clinton Road. That house was our daughter's house. Our niece wanted to do her own thing, but we had her back. The business was doing good, and everyone was great. Now the house was completed. My wife was coming home in two days. We were throwing a homecoming party for their safe return home. The grandbaby was so happy about the trip. She never knew where she was going until she got there. They hugged me so tight. I and my wife had talked about sitting back and letting our grandbaby run the restaurant for a straight week after school.

My wife had been keeping an eye on the baby girl. Wifey thought the baby had her way. She was so well-liked in school in ASBS, she was well-*mannered* at school and home, but she also had that mean side in her. My wife said one day last week at the store, a man had come in putting some beer inside his coat. My granddaughter had come around the corner with a baseball bat, making him put it down and get out of the store. My wife was in *shock*, saying not a word. Grandbaby went back to work like nothing had happened. My wife said she was so proud of her because she knew for sure that was her baby girl. Also, if something happened to us, she would keep our lives and business going.

I just came up with a new contract at the gas company doing all the employees' cars every Friday. So I wanted to surprise my girls by sending them out to Hawaii for a week. My daughter couldn't make it, so I asked our niece to go. She was going. My wife's eyes at this time were acting crazy on her, but she was okay. This time she came home, we were making her go to Cleveland Clinic for testing. Without her, there was nothing. She was everyone's backbone.

Her sisters had just opened up their own hair and nail shop out on St. Clair 156th Street. Why up there? I didn't know. Maybe because it was one ride from their home. I could feel a little *jealousy* from them about me taking good care of their sister, but their sister had been my ride or die from day one, and that's how it would be. My wife, my life, my world.

So many questions had been asked, why was I *treating* her granddaughter like mine, or should I say my daughter? We had come up fucked up, and it was life or death; she had no father. She didn't have a father; he got killed after she was born, being in the wrong place at the wrong time. She was thirteen years old, in the sixth grade, about to go to the seventh grade. I and my wife and her mom were renting her the biggest limo ever, a Hummer limo for her and her friends with money in her pocket. After they kicked it, it was a party at the house for just her class. I wasn't going to be there. Her oldest cousin, my nephew, and his friend, my wife, and my daughter were trippin', but you only live once. Trust me, it was mostly all girls. It was crazy, at $2,500 a night, nothing but the best, and that it was. Even my wife and daughter felt young. The video was crazy, them dancing like women.

The next day, we learned that some young kid got killed, and shot over a dice game on the corner of my wife's store. He was nineteen years old.

I and my nephew had been talking about renting a boat and going out in the middle of the lake to fish, my second time, his first time. It had been raining for a week. Right after that, we were going to have a ball. They helped you catch fish and clean them. I was thinking about a big church fish fry.

Speaking of church, my wife was looking at the empty field across the street for $400. That would be for the store get-togethers. And nephew was doing good with the power wash and holding his family and home down. I heard he was hustling a little weed—that was cool, just nothing hard. In disbelief, we had caught over three hundred pounds of perch, catfish, and walleye. It was all clean, ready to go into the grease. Wifey was happy to have fresh fish for her church dinners.

The birthday of the father of my daughter's baby was today, so I had to take my grandbaby out for ice cream or something to make her smile. She knew her father somewhat from pictures and stories from her mother, who was my first love. Still, there was no one in her life but God and her baby and work.

Looking into my life, I was grateful for letting God into it and changing it. Even though I was still in the same streets, I could see the change in the hood. Empty houses were still there, but worse. Buildings had been going down more, people were using drugs more, street corners were getting fuller, and more young people were hanging out. Most people were just afraid of losing what they had or getting killed by someone trying to take their hard-earned things, food, or the house they still had, even though it was two families in one house.

From seeing this every day, my wife and I took a few people daily and offered them a little work to put money in their pockets. Before we threw away food, we gave it away, trying to help at least one person out of the crowd. My wife had also been thinking of getting a building nearby to restore and make into a shelter, and getting help from the state in doing it. Her church was behind her, just finding the right neighborhood and location was the holdup. It got really cold in the winter. Most people from around here were sleeping in abandoned houses with their kids. That hurt. They were able-bodied but didn't know what was wrong with them—no job training or home training. Some were young parents, babies having babies, with no money from welfare or help. The fathers were dead, in prison, or on drugs. The food centers were closing down in the hoods, and even the scrap game was getting harder. Now you needed a car just to get in the yard, and they paid you in check form.

It was funny because there was nowhere to live for most people, and looking at hard times, drug hustlers were still making nice money out in the streets. How could you do drugs with nowhere to live or nothing to eat? Wow. I was just happy at the end of the day that we were okay and keeping the faith of the Lord. Remember that this was the neighborhood that we grew up in, went to most of the same schools, and I knew most of the people in this area. Things had changed over the years.

Last week, I heard of a man who was found dead inside an old house. He had been inside for a week and a few days before anyone found him, but in the hood, no one was missing anyway. It was someone from this area. It was the old owner of the tire shop across the street. He had frozen to death. He had his hands in a lot when I was a kid. Now, without any family, what were they going to do? Rumors were that he had lived there for a long time, years. Wow. Shortly after his death, the police reached the house for other clues and found over 19,000 gold coins dated back to the 1900s, two pocket watches, and over $100,000 in cash. That must have been the money from when he sold his shop. He had a wife and two kids. She died shortly after they had their kids from cancer. His sisters and brother lived out in LA somewhere. His kids may have lived out that way as well, but it was sad that no one would take care of his funeral. No one hardly knew him from back in the day. This is why I was living my life as if it were my last, one day at a time.

I also had a wonderful wife who loved me for me, and a graceful, beautiful daughter and a granddaughter. Hopefully, when it is time, my granddaughter could and would take everything over. On one sunny day at the store, my family was all there cooking, having a good time when they saw a man in black, tall and heavyset, walk in looking like death was in him. He asked for me, scaring everyone. They told him I was out and about. He smiled with dark and dirty teeth and walked out. They followed, looking for his car. There was no car. He just disappeared after two or three steps into the street. Wow.

Being in deep disbelief in the back of my mind, I wondered if I should be worried or afraid that this could be my past coming to haunt me again. A few days and weeks went by, and no one knew or saw anything. My nephew's friend, whom he was dealing with, got caught up with two pounds and $60,000 in his car, telling on everyone that he was in contact with. My nephew's name was the first one on his list because he wanted my nephew out of the way. He wanted my nephew's wife and lifestyle. The police never said anything to my nephew, and that dude was never seen or heard from again. The feds got him, the hood guessed. And that man who came to the store? That was a longtime friend from the Fortieth projects who used to chase kids going and coming from school. His name was the

Capman. That man was the East ghost, especially in the Woodland area. Man, he used to scare White people, getting them that good. The police had him a lot of times in handcuffs, and he still got away with the cuffs on. He was a track star. Carl Lewis couldn't keep up with him.

But don't get it twisted; in my hood, this shit went hard, and crackheads got it in. The crime rate was high. I did my thing. Those motherfuckers would use their pros and cons all day, every day. We just blocked that shit out and lived. Speaking of living, I set up a camping trip for my family in June, two months away from now. Some dude called me for a car wash yesterday. I got there just to see that he had just been shot in the arm. He wanted the blood off his car door.

On the other side of the street lay a man also with a gunshot to the head, dead. He tried to rob him—in self-defense. Fuck! $50 for a quick-ass wash. That's more money for food or something for the trip. Everyone was bringing their own food if they wanted to, but I was paying for everything. This would be the last family get-together outing for the year. My wife was getting sick; her eyes were losing sight, and there was a small cancer in her liver. I was taking her everywhere she wanted before that happened.

We had been together since high school. I couldn't lose her; she was my rib bone. So I was going to retire as well and close down the stores and sell them. This was why the camping trip was so important. My wife's church family was by her side. At this point, everyone agreed that our grandbaby was the one who needed to be watched. That was our heart. She was fifteen years old now. If she wanted everything, she could have it when she turned twenty-one and was done with school, with no kids. That was the rule. The apartments would pay the taxes on everything, the stores, and our house.

At this time, the family was trying, crying, hugging, and praying. Her nephew was hurt as well. He would help his cousin run the family business, and God would run his course. The last person in my life was going, and I couldn't stop life from passing. I prayed more than I ever did. Her family was family, but not mine. I would be a loner once again. On August 13, 2019, my wife passed away in her sleep next to me at home. It was a hard feeling to feel, but her church family was there, supporting me and the family.

We had been sitting on those guys who got my nephew for those two ounces and $1,500. There was an empty building in the hood that people used for dumping trash or smoking crack. That was a perfect place to take them. We had gotten some strippers from Magic City to take them to a motel room on Euclid. Inside, we would be there with masks on, acting as if we were robbing the whole set, dog-walking the strippers for money, beating the guys, and putting them inside the truck, beating them on the way to the building. The truck was stolen from Sandusky. Blood was everywhere. No one knew shit, just the strippers. They were good. The money we took, we gave back to them, sending them on their way, keeping their mouths closed.

We took off our masks. Their faces were in shock. For streets away, no one could hear them screaming for help. It was too late for that sorry shit. Both dead. After two days of beating, we cut their hands off and put them on their mother's porch. Their bodies were also cut up into pieces and put out of town.

Pictures were all over the news and the paper for weeks. The case remained a cold case for years. It stayed like that until this year. Someone was looking hard before knocking down that building, finding DNA of their blood, and people started talking shit about what they were doing before the murders—robberies. That was when the hood was saying that my nephew was hit by them last and that I was crazy and known for killing people. The FBI and local police took us in for questions and let us go after a day in jail but could never break our story. They took our DNA, which takes a few weeks to come back.

In the meantime, it was time to get a good-ass lawyer and keep on living. We went late to burn down that building, trying to keep them from looking around more. It worked for a while, but someone was always seeing something that didn't need to be seen. Trust that someone came forward, saying they saw us coming out of the building running in black clothes.

Those people were running their mouths. I had to get my dude from Fortieth, the "Caveman," the man who came inside the store, to paint those people for us for $50,000. Afterward, we sent him out of town for ten years, paying him something soft like $800 monthly. There was nothing they could go on. The case went back cold, and the body parts were never found.

That was the first time my nephew had gone gangster. I stopped drinking shortly after that, doing my old lifestyle, living, washing cars, keeping the stores open, and keeping my wife's memories alive. My grandbaby still, to this day, was like my wife. She had her way completely. She knew me inside and out.

This story got more fucked up. Those two strippers were pulled out of the lake last night with gunshots to the head. No one knew anything about that. It wasn't my work. Someone they got from the club they were working at killed them, some light-skinned dude with a truck with gold Ds on it.

Shit was about to get real around this place. My niece and daughter were just coming out of Planet Fitness on W Twenty-Fifth around 10:15 a.m. one morning and were confronted by two niggas with masks on, jumping out of an old black truck, putting them inside, and taking off, leaving a ransom note saying they wanted $100,000 and the title to my businesses, or their body parts would be spread across Cleveland. Man, my mind was blown, tripping. Everyone was talking good, but I wasn't hearing anything. I had no other choice but to dig up my crazy-ass foster brother, who loved drama like I did. It had been years since we spoke. I hoped he was still alive and able. It was on. Steve answered. It was on. I was about to send for his plane ticket to Cleveland and get his boy from the army to come too.

The kidnappers kept calling with that bullshit. My family was crying, tripping, and afraid. Deep down this time, I was too, but I couldn't show any fear. We didn't know what was what or why me. I went and got my little brother and friend. The family was tripping.

The first time hearing and seeing him amazed me with how much we looked alike, somewhat like twins. I showed my brother the ransom note and the voicemails from the kidnappers, trying to put two and two together and looking for the reasons, drinking some vodka and ice. He asked me who her last boyfriend was and who his family was. That was something I never asked or got into with her lifestyle. I always trusted her. But why were you asking? And who were the dudes your sister's in-laws were seeing? Once again, I didn't know. That's when they said that's where we should start. It might be an inside job, someone I knew who knew too much about me and had been watching me for a while. Snoop. This might be true.

Now we had to have a hidden place in the middle of nowhere to tutor these people. It was a lot, and it was about to be a lot of killing and body parts in Cleveland. I got another note on my apartment door when all of us were about to come out. Really, this close to me without hearing anything.

Mt. Stani Church on Woodland would be holding her funeral on August 17 at 9:00 a. m. Cleveland was welcome. I was taking it hard, but I was doing okay. I just wanted to be alone, really. I could still smell her around me, hearing her voice, the laughs, and her telling me to stop when I did something crazy. Her touch, mainly. She was going to be missed.

Our daughter just came in, taking it harder than me, her, and my grandbaby. I had to be the strength for them. Her sister was staying to help around the house. My daughter was stopping her career for now to run the stores with her cousin and daughter, a family together. I was proud of that. My heart had been broken forever. Flowers and roses were everywhere. My wife touched a lot of people. Things she did I never knew. For the community, I was aware, but paying it forward, I never knew, which was good. If she were here, I would hug her so tight in pride. The happiest man in the world she made me.

Everyone was trying their hardest to hold it down. My nephew was taking it hard. He was giving out too much love to the wrong people. He got set up for a robbery on Bonna for two ounces and $1,500 by his supposed niggas. People had been trying to break into the store from the back wall. The other restaurant was cool. For the first time, I was going to cook a pig in the ground. I, an old school from down south, just have something different to do. I was back drinking beer. The pain was still fresh. My niece was holding her schooling down and still coming to work, running things like it never happened, as if my wife was coming through that door soon. Her sister often tripped on the same feelings. Maybe it was her spirit in here. The pig was smelling up the street. People were coming from everywhere, asking when it was going to be done. A pig in the ground took over a day and night to turn slowly, getting drunk doing it.

We were looking around for infrared beams on our bodies while walking around, checking for bombs inside cars and around the building. The note said, "Come alone with no police at the Burger King on Fifty-Fifth at 1:00 p.m. today." My brother lay back across the street at McDonald's, and his boy was inside an old car with an AK watching my back. I went inside and sat, waiting for someone to walk up. No one showed. But looking down at a napkin, there was another ransom notice. It said, "You're not alone like I asked you to come." Now I was thinking this shit was real. Who the fuck was this?

It had been a week and no word if they were alive or anything. Getting inside my brother's car, my cell phone rang as we were riding down Superior. My daughter and niece were crying, begging for me to save them. The phone died. I and my brother were in wonder, like, "Fuck! What are we going to do?" So we were about to start taking her boyfriend's family to the trap building to question them all one by one.

Starting with the mother, stripping her clothes, putting gas all over her body, cigarette burns all over her face, beating her with locks in the socks—this went on until she said something. On the other side, her husband was getting the same but with a broomstick in his ass while she watched it going on. He was also beaten with locks in the sock, a steel bed frame he was tied up to with a battery and wire to his dick, pouring water on him, making him talk. Their son, we had him in the middle of the room naked, also with a broomstick the same as his father. No one said anything. After two days of this, we had to let them go after we shot them up with 90 percent heroin, which should have made them lose their minds, so no one would talk.

Now the boyfriend of my sister's in-law kicked in the door at 4:00 a.m. We even paid crackheads for information. Nothing was popping up. We were wasting time, and still no word from the kidnappers.

A female arm was left inside the wall of my building with a message saying some crazy shit: "You need to come this time, or they will die." The meeting place was the Randall Mall parking lot, the east lot, at 8:00 p.m. "You will see a black truck. Bring the money and the titles of your business. Do this, and your family will be released." We didn't know who these people were or where they were from, only that they were crazier than we were. My family, at this time, was in fear. I had to do this, but now they knew every GPS. Maybe a small tracker inside the briefcase and one inside the money. If this was done right, my family would be returned, and we could find out who was behind this bullshit.

The meeting went down, but I had my brother on top of the roof with an AK, and his boy inside the trunk of the car with an AK and a bomb. I took the money in the middle of the car; the lights were blinding me. I could hear my daughter and niece crying for me. A man in black clothes and black glasses—I couldn't tell if he was Black or White.

My family ran toward me, happy. The man slowly got inside his car and took off. I saw about three people inside. The hugs were tight as hell. They said the men never touched them sexually or anything. I called my family with the good news. Everyone was happy for their safe return. The hood was like family at the building, in joy. The church family, everyone—tears were falling off our faces as well. Yeah, men can cry.

My nephew just pulled my coattail, saying that it could be the mob boys from Miles behind this. I asked, "What proof do you have?" He said, "It's downstairs waiting." He had a naked man on a pole. In disbelief of his role in the kidnapping, he was one of the ones with the gun, putting them inside the truck. The other people—it's too late to look back and say sorry. We waited until the next day when everyone was out doing their thing. Coming from Fifty-Fifth, we ended first. The man was still naked. We dragged him down the street until he was dead, then put him in a field and watched him burn.

That didn't bring anything but more drama to the table. We kept our business running as normal. I just put some killers with my family, inside and outside, more young folks that just got blessed in. The FBI and the police asked crazy-ass questions, but no one said a word. The church, I couldn't believe, understood my actions and prayed for us. Snipers were on the top of each building just for the getaway if shit jumped off.

Meanwhile, we knew what we were going to do now. This guy told us who to look for, where to go, and the reasons. It was the old man's son who was a crackhead. Remember from the beginning? This shit was back. The guy was up on Murray Hill alone, sitting by a store, drinking coffee and eating donuts around 9:00 to 10:30 a.m. every morning. So we did a day ride to watch the setup. The dude was on the money. The dead man was there. The question was where we were going to take and do with this bitch. Meanwhile, we were sending my nephew out of town to bring the old boy back from LA. That $800-a-month shit for nothing—we were going to mix and match his ass with this bitch's body.

This guy's plane was arriving in Cleveland soon, so we were going to keep him close. My sister-in-law thought that the pig cook-out might be another great idea for the store, so that's what we were going to do. Kidnap this bitch from that storefront in the morning, keeping both of them alive until we got to Detroit. I called a friend out there with a backhoe and asked him to dig a hole like eight feet deep. We were going to cut both of them up, keeping their heads on ice until we got to Kentucky. We were going to feed their heads to the pigs and watch them enjoy their food from Cleveland. The other dude that kidnapped my family, that's the motherfucker I wanted. He dealt with my daughter and niece, and I was going to sit back and watch the *movie*. He was hiding out up the hill in Morse Black Projects, easy prey. Some pussy would bring him out to lay.

We got the perfect face for the job—my niece he kidnapped, something to scare his ass. We had her be herself, walking around with the other girls, kicking it. He saw her, almost ran, shitting on himself, running right into my nephew's hands. My nephew put the

9 mm to his head, wanting to kill him badly. I said just in time, the smell of shit burning our noses.

Looking around my uncle's farm for the first time in a long time felt good, enjoying the fresh air and the cooking. You talk about good steak. Man, you could smell it from miles away. His cabin was just open, no locks, no one around for miles. The water was so, so good. It was the best in the world, spring water. He took us hunting for food. It was peaceful to kill a turkey or deer, to see how to clean the animal, to cure the food, and the right way to freeze it. The cows and pig lots were interesting as well, a lot different from city life. No gunshots, no crowds anywhere, no nothing. I thought of dropping off a good few dollars to buy myself a setup. After this shit, I would need to do something.

I had been thinking about just letting everyone run the business for a year, just to get away from the city, and I wanted to get close to my wife's *spirit*. Too much drama. I was in my sixties now, and getting sick. I wasn't saying anything to anyone. I needed to talk to the graveyard people to be laid next to my wife. When I got home, I would talk to my daughter about my ideas and my illness. I believed it was cancer.

It's time to come home. The meat was cured and frozen enough for the trip. Uncle's farm was peaceful; we all enjoyed the stay. The family was talking, everything was okay. Just a black car had been sitting across the street watching the stores and then driving off. Some said they were taking pictures. I thought it might be the feds or local police, investigating me, looking for a case to get me on.

The church family was so ready for the cookout. I still couldn't believe the love and support they had given us. My wife would have been happy and proud of our daughter, niece, and grandbaby. Our grandbaby was holding on strong, still going through school and working hard in my wife's name. We just pulled up with the meat, and also this nigga in the truck, taped up and knocked out. Everyone had to be inside the store so we could take this bitch downstairs. My daughter didn't know what was in store for her yet. We took him down, dragging him headfirst, taping him to a pole naked with his underwear on. My seat was in the corner. My brother and his crew would help when needed, which I *doubted*.

I just sent my daughter downstairs for some pop so she could see that bitch and see her reaction. She came back to me with a smile on her face, saying not much of anything. I told her to tell her cousin to do the same thing, which she did. She went downstairs, the same kind of reaction on her face. The church members were having fun for once. Everyone was acting like people and not just for God. They were drinking; the pastor was playing and singing R&B songs. We had the pig in the ground, and the girls were in the kitchen prepping the food: deer meat and pieces of the cow and pig, country-style cooking. The hood loved their setup dinners.

Downstairs, I set a knife set on the table, locks in the socks, a bucket of water with a wire to a battery to shock his ass, and gasoline. They were downstairs loving this shit—the new blood of the Williams family *killers*. The pastor was about drunk, drinking that country corn liquor, turning the pig. I was sitting there with him, my nephew, my brother, and his friend. Meanwhile, my niece and daughter were downstairs, taking turns fucking dude up. The police were still outside, looking in as best they could. I loved it because they couldn't touch any of us for shit. I would send them a plate over when it got done. The hole was ready for his ass. I got a big bag of lime to cover him with.

The next morning, I and the pastor were still outside cooking the pig. My brother and his boy took the bitch, and put him in a stolen truck with a trash bag over his head. He was slowly begging for his life. Everyone else was upstairs sleeping. They got his ass there, shooting him in the head between the eyes and watching his body fall into the hole. It was over. Now the lime and dirt, and two streets over, they burned the truck. Getting into my nephew's truck, I had to admit that my nephew had the heart in all of this. I couldn't believe it but was proud of them all. The church was also unbelievable too— they were human too.

The pastor had asked me why I was so evil. My answer was, "I do to others as they do to me. I love God. I respect the Lord's work, but the devil is a fight every day."

Just as I said, I sent over a plate of food to the police officers with some cold pop and water. Their faces were red as hell. The hood was all over the place, eating and drinking, playing cards, and listening to music. The feds had something else in *mind*. The next morning, after everyone had left the party, they came to take me in for a lot of unanswered questions and almost had a good enough reason to keep me for murder and money laundering in the F3 area, but it couldn't hold. I called my daughter to come and get me from St. Clair downtown, which was good because now we could talk in peace.

I told her about my cancer and wanting to sell the corner store and move out of town with her uncle in Kentucky for my resting place. I had been a thug my whole life and a killer, which she knew as a kid. People talked, she said. My blood was in her now. She had the touch of blood. The police for now were down. The hood was back together, normal.

My grandbaby wasn't a baby anymore. She had just finished high school and was about to go to college like her mother, with no kids. My wife would be so proud right now. After everything that happened during the years around here, my daughter said, "Sell it all, Daddy, and we all move to Kentucky. Everyone came when you called, and everyone is going to listen and move to Daddy. We were just waiting on you."

Right now, everything that we owned and had was worth $2.5 million. My nephew and his wife were feeling the same. His mother was saying the same, and the last sister, the baby, had been ready to go. The houses they had they still owned down south, which made it good for us. My house was just about getting done. It would be the new state-of-the-art log cabin. *Flip Flip* tint on my windows that goes with the day, never can see in, just out. Two whirlpools, three bedrooms, a bearskin rug all over my house, touch screen registration, all stainless steel, an eighty-inch TV on the wall, a pool table, an upgraded bar, and leather furniture.

I just talked to the pastor again about the amount, and we came up with $1.3 million now and $1.2 million later in three years, which will be in my daughter's and niece's names. My granddaughter will also have a part of that pie. Moving from Cleveland, for four families, it will cost $8,300 on the Mayflower truck all at one time, which is good. We were all getting out *safely*. The tenants over the store—the pastor was happy that they were good tenants, so they *continued* to stay as they paid $450 *monthly*. They would run both stores as is. The police could now leave and stop messing with people. The hood would be missed. I was even thinking of bringing my wife's body with me so that when my time came, we could be laid to rest together.

Everyone was packed and happy, ready to roll, food, drink, and gas up, and not looking back. The freeway speed limit was sixty-five miles per hour. We were gone. *Deuces, peace*—hood rich, we were out.

Getting outside of Cleveland, the air began to smell so, so good, different, as if you could smell the farm life already. We saw cows, horses, and farms, all on open land. It was my dream—I finally got it—a piece of the American dream. I called Uncle just to double-check on things. It was all at 90 percent. My cabin would be done in two weeks, which was good. I would be with him on the land to even it more. The things I would keep inside a pod that was waiting for us.

My nephew and his kids were happy because his kids had never been down south, my granddaughter too. She was a little unhappy about leaving her friends. She would be okay later; they could visit and do that Facebook thing. My wife had made a promise that when she finished high school and went to college, we would buy her a drop-top car. She was into Saabs. Now a bright red drop-top 2020 Saab was waiting in the driveway for her. No one knew. My wife was smiling from up above. It was never the same without you, Boo.

Uncle took me everywhere with him, proud. You could see the happiness in him. He took me to a barn party—like a pig roasting over an open fire, a goat also over the fire. People knew I wasn't from there from the way I talked and dressed. The women were all over me. I danced with a few but couldn't kick it. Uncle pulled me to the side, saying, "Son, I respect you for taking good care of my niece and my family. You are a man. Also, son, you are human. My niece has been gone for over six years. You have to let go of her and live."

Later, I asked my daughter and her sisters about me moving on with my life in a friendship with someone else. Hell, I was of age, but the thought really wasn't on my mind. Their answer was, "Daddy, that's on you." My wife's sisters were a little uneasy about it. To them, that was like cheating. My heart and soul would always belong to their sister. I wished I was on her side right now. Then it all came out about my illness.

My cancer was progressing fast. My dream of getting my wife's body down here—I was sending for her to be placed on my land in front of my cabin where I would lie next to her. We did this together. We had been together for forty years. The American love story was us. It felt funny being here—no fights in the streets, no crowds, nothing for miles, no neighbor right next door, just fresh air and God over your shoulder.

Her uncle was setting up the plane to bring my wife down *tomorrow*. He and I were digging the hole and doing the surrounding area. We both wanted something special for her. A rose garden would be placed around her, and white roses would be the *fence* on a white fence. It would be nice and peaceful for her. And I could always sit and talk to her now, taking her soul with me every step. The river was right up the walk. My cabin was together now, but I was alone in peace. My family was doing their thing—working, school, and living. This was my life—*hunting* and *relaxing* around my cabin. My man *cave*, I guessed. There wasn't even a plane flying around. Just sometimes. My grandbaby was happy with her new car. They said she was crying with happiness. That made me feel good. I could feel her hand on my shoulder and her voice inside my ear, "I love you, baby!"

The pastor had told me the love we shared was unbreakable, not that easy to break. So be happy to have that much. Some people don't have that, my son.

A piece of fried steak or chicken tasted so good, and the smell would take you off your feet. The eggs tasted different out here. I had been keeping up with my brother and his boy. His boy got shot in the leg and arm during an attempted carjacking when they hit Detroit's 8 Mile. Even my brother said he was doing okay and that they were working at a BBQ spot. That was some good shit out there.

Besides drugs, food out there was a big-ass *seller*. My nephew was still power-washing cars and landscaping out here. My daughter and niece were back in college, and doing good. Their moms were now doing hair again out of their houses, which was great. This was the best move we ever made.

I needed to find something to do. I couldn't hide forever. I was looking around town and downtown to see what types of businesses they had here. My nephew said that landscaping, painting houses, and building houses were the only businesses here that made money besides drugs. So I started riding with my nephew, seeing how it worked. He was doing the damn thing.

Not being funny, but out here, I saw nothing but money. There were a lot of bars, strip clubs, and storefronts, but hardly any BBQ spots. I thought of a carwash with a BBQ spot inside, with women in their swimsuits washing cars and making the food. Or a BBQ spot with a strip club, with LED lights. However they called them, that light up the *brass* hit hard, with four poles for the strippers, food, and strippers. It could work. I opened my mouth to my nephew about my idea. He agreed that this might be something to keep me busy and get me a small place in the city to watch my spot. And go to the hills to rest. This might work out for me. There was only one small problem that could stop that dream: my liquor license from Ohio. Could I use them? He said, "Maybe, do it anyway."

So I started looking for the perfect spot. I found one right next to an old carwash. It was a drive-through; it just needed to be upgraded. I bought both the carwash and the building next door for my *restaurant* and club. Now I needed some good detail guys to fix up my club first.

Both buildings I got for $67,755. That was nice. Now interviewing contractors with my ideas, one said that it would cost me about $30,000 to do the bar and $25,000 for the *materials*. I wanted lights all on the bar, the walls, and the bar itself that *blink* when the *brass* hits, and a two-way *mirror* in my office and behind the bar so I could watch the bartender. Also, I wanted a *secret* wall that took me from anywhere inside or outside to my car ASAP. Since that was extra, it cost $15,000 more. I agreed.

The work was getting done. Meanwhile, I was looking for cooks and strippers. The strippers had to be twenty-one years old, and my cooks would be selling lobster, shrimp, crab legs, everything. All that was VIP to get inside my club. You would pay $5 at the door. The max number of people it could hold was three hundred at a time, and drinks started at $5 a shot. The music would be Cleveland style because their music here was different from ours. I would have the best state-of-the-art cameras all over my businesses, the ones that showed an ant crawl and what color it was. Hiring signs would be posted soon for everything, and the security would be college boys. This way, they knew just about everyone in town. The strippers would be paying $300 a night for the spotlight and for their safety as well. The first six drinks for them only would be free.

It was a drug-free place, but in my VIP rooms, it went hard. The see-out window tint only, with a big-ass screen TV, and an open bar. The price went up when the drinks changed, starting at $150. I wanted twelve security guards, three-strip poles, the cameras, crazy-ass liquor, two guards at the front doors, and a box office to pay to get in. The place would have guns inside. Open hours would be from 6:00 p.m. to 3:30 a.m. Monday through Saturday. Food would be open from 10:00 a.m. until 12:30 p.m. Monday through Saturday.

I guessed I was praying that my sisters-in-law would come back and work for me. It would be their business like before. I didn't want any money, just love, and to see them get paid too in my wife's name. Everyone was back on the team. It was about to be on like the old days but a lot better, with no *enemies*. My brother and his boy were like, "Hell yeah, bro, it's on. Just call if you need me."

We were all happy, even down to the new strippers, because that was cheap to them. The college boys were about to break down my door for the work, at $15 an hour starting. I wanted the *restaurant* to open up first for a week before anything else. My nephew, that was his, just paid the bills. My sisters-in-law, the same thing. And my club was all mine. This way, everyone would have a piece of the pie.

My sister was trying to put it in my head about that old ice cream shop up the street. It needed a little work, but it was in a good spot. Maybe my grandbaby could run it for the summer break, she and her cousin. That would put money in their pockets for school. I asked them what they thought about it. They said yes and asked when it would be open. I told them I would buy it for them and have it fixed up by next week. "What color do you want it to be?"

"Yellow, that's a good color."

I needed to ask my sisters about that. They wanted red and white. Me, I wanted the inside to be all gray and black.

The first real night would be October 18, my birthday. In the meantime, I had it open for the strippers to practice their acts and open for business. My first week was slow, but my gross was $8,500. The word needed to get out, so I made some flyers and put them on the radio. This was on a Tuesday. People slowly started coming in, getting food, and seeing how nice my club was. When Friday night came, man, it was on. People from all over came to the place.

Money was falling so hard in my safe that I needed two of them. The restaurant was running out of food. We grossed probably about $65,000 that one night. The strippers were so happy. They made out nicely, all twelve of them, and that wasn't even the grand opening. We all had to triple up on *shock* for sure. The carwash had not stopped yet. It was still going right now. A perfect-ass idea in a perfect place.

My daughter asked me, "Daddy, if you started dating, would it be a young girl or someone in your age range?"

I said, "Why? I never thought of that yet, but why?"

"Her teacher from school wanted to meet you. She's in your age range, has two grown kids, a grandmother. Her husband died like Mom around the same time. And I am tired of seeing you lonely."

I said, "Now you are sounding like your uncle. Okay, tell her to meet me tomorrow at the restaurant at 1:00 p.m. I have to set up the hole for a pig."

Seasoning my pig, I was busy working when I remembered her teacher was coming to meet me. I saw a nice white drop-top pull up in the parking lot. A sexy lady got out and entered the door, looking around. I said, "Hi, can I help you?"

She replied, "I'm looking for Mr. Williams."

I said, "That's me." It felt like I was a kid again and couldn't talk. I offered her something to drink. She sat down, watching me prepare the food. She was amazed to see a man cook like I was.

I got the pig going, the half cow slowly cooking, along with the goat. That smell of the South could bring the dead alive. I mean, it smelled good. So far, we were connecting, touching hands, and she was smiling. But in the back of my mind, I wondered, why me? So I asked, "It's just that I'm from Cleveland, Ohio, and you want to show me around on your side?" That Sunday night, things were slow, so I closed early. I called her, and she came. We rode around and parked at a lake or ocean, watching the stars and the moon, and asking questions about our states. It was nice and peaceful. I respected her as a woman all that night.

She asked me on another date, this time at her house. What was crazy was I didn't know how to get there, but I said yes. I could use my GPS system to get there. Things worked out for the following Sunday. I didn't open on Sundays anyway, and there wasn't a pig cooking. My daughter picked me up and showed me how to get there in her car. Her car rode good. My wife would be happy that we had a *beautiful* smart daughter. She told me that her teacher really did like me a lot, but I asked, "Why? Is it my money?"

She said, "No, she has money, Daddy. You'll see it tonight. I promise she's rich too."

I had my nephew shine up my truck and put some long-lasting air freshener in there. I washed my ass real good. I got to her door just at seven thirty like she asked me. She was in a nice, sexy blue dress showing everything. It had been years since I had any sex, and that's what she said as well. I was going to hold down my thoughts and respect tonight. She made some porterhouse steaks with a shrimp salad and potatoes, with red table wine and candlelight, and the fireplace burning. At this point, I was speechless as hell.

The dinner was good. We were talking, and connecting well. She went inside her room and changed clothes, coming out in a nightgown looking sexy as hell, everything showing. She smelled like a rose. I was sitting on the corner of the couch, thinking, *Damn*, but I had to respect just a little longer. She lay down in my arms.

We kept talking through the night. She asked me why I came to Kentucky. I answered, "After my wife's death, I needed to be close to where she was from. Her family is from here as well, so it's what it is." She understood my feelings. Her waist was inside my hands, and her head down on my leg like a pillow, driving me crazy on the inside for real.

I asked if she had ever ridden a horse before. She said it had been a long time, probably when she was a little girl. So next week-end, after work, I was going to take her to my farm to ride and cook out like a *picnic* on the riverside of my property. I had been asking my wife to forgive me and forget me for my cheating around her private arm. It must have been okay because I never felt any crazy feelings inside my heart about us.

As I showed her around my farm, I explained that my wife and I worked hard for this and that everything wasn't always easy for us. She said my daughter told her some good and bad times that we all had shared. Being amazed at how my farm looked so great, it was crazy. I had been there for like six months and not one murder or police chase down the street. It was peaceful here. She said everyone here was peaceful and loving.

She spent the night with me at the farm, enjoying the *whirlpool* naked together. We made love until the next morning and slept until noon. We were both late for work. My nephew had the keys to open up the club, but she was a teacher. That looked bad, but it was cool. My daughter covered for her. She took over her classes so we could spend the day together more.

So we rode the horses around through the mountains, *admiring* the views that nature had. Man, the sights were nice. Later that day, we even made fishing poles and made a fire, cooked fish, and slept again together on the riverside. Spending time with her was getting too good to be true. The next morning, we were up for work. We both agreed that it might be time to have our families meet. I thought that was a great idea because our friendship was taking off nicely. So I thought about the *restaurant* patio that my nephew had just enclosed, with a firepit in the middle. I would have the butcher cut up some two-and-a-half T-bone steaks and some porterhouse steaks, and my sister-in-law would prepare the dinner. Since he had run the club that day, I gave him the earnings of $18,000. The strippers got a piece of that pie too—all got $300,000 apiece.

Tina—that's her name—the teacher, agreed for this weekend, Sunday night at 7:00 p.m. This way, everyone could show up, and my business would be closed—no crowds around. Her son and daughter were nice. They were my daughter's age. Her daughter and my niece were in classes together, which was nice, and her son did landscaping. My nephew knew him.

Everyone seemed happy for us except my wife's little sister and my granddaughter, who was now twenty-five years old. They grew fast. Wow. They thought I would let her take my wife's place. No one could, but I was happy today with Tina.

Tina and I left and rode around town before coming to my farm. She had never spent time on a farm like this, she said. I asked her how long she had been teaching and when she planned to retire. She had been teaching for over fifteen years and would retire whenever she wanted. "Why?" she asked. Tina was fifty-one years old, and I was sixty-one. With the way things were looking, I would have money for everyone for a long time. She had a few dollars saved up. I was thinking about living together on the farm to see if it would work. She was okay with that. She could keep her house, just lock it up, keep teaching this year, and retire next year, so we could travel across the world by train.

"On a train?" she asked.

"Yes, my grown ass is afraid of flying," I said.

She laughed and said, "I am too. So if the bus or train can't take us, then it wasn't meant to be."

Still, no one knew about my cancer except my daughter. So we sneaked and went to the doctor together. I was doing okay for now, just needed to stay away from stress and stay in the fresh air. I wanted to tell my nephew, but he might take it too hard. He was like a son to me. My daughter believed that too. I wanted a lawyer to come as well. I wanted my nephew to keep the carwash, my sisters-in-law to keep the *restaurant*, my daughter and niece to have the ice cream shop, and my nephew and daughter to be partners in the club. Tina could have 20 percent of the club if we married. I also wanted my house in the city for my daughter and niece, $500,000 apiece, and $500,000 for Tina, with $50,000 a year. The family could all share my cabin, and my last request was to lay my body next to my wife in front of my farm.

I was really thinking about stepping down—no, I was stepping down from the club and giving it to my nephew, asking for 20 percent a month in gross pay, somewhere like $50,000 or something comfortable. "I am sick with cancer and don't have that long to live, nephew, so this has to be this way. Understand, you are a man, you can handle this."

I called Tina. She was preparing a lovely dinner for me, happy with a *glow* on her face. My daughter loved her as if she were her mother. I asked Tina to join me on a three-day *cruise* on the river. It took off at three thirty the next day. I also wanted her to put in her retirement papers. This was when I planned to make love to her and ask her to marry me. The captain of the boat and his crew were preparing a nice three-day cruise for us. We would have the time of our lives, dancing, drinking, and eating whatever she wanted. The sky was the limit. After this, I wanted to go on a helicopter ride to face that fear somewhat—me in the air, yeah, right. If we could do this, we could go everywhere money could take us. But I had to break Tina's heart with this bad news. Now was never the right time, but it had to be.

"Tina, baby, I'm feeling you too much. I want to spend the rest of my life with you, but I have cancer."

She sat there with tears in her eyes and asked, "How long do you have?"

The doctor said maybe three or four years. I also explained to her that I was leaving her my house in the city and a lot of money. What was crazy was that she and I wanted a baby together. We would need a good doctor to help us, but the good news was it could be done. It cost like $25,000. We set it up without anyone knowing anything, and it came true. We were having a baby. A few weeks before seeing the doctor again, it was good news. He approved it. Now yes, we were having a baby. A sixty-two-year-old man becoming a father. Wow. Tina was in her fifties. Wow. Just think what everybody was going to say. My daughter was going to be a big sister. Wow. Everyone was going to trip.

My wife never wanted any more kids; to her, once was enough. Tina's daughter, my nephew, and my daughter were planning the wedding. My daughter was coming with a big surprise herself. I was going to call the pastor myself with the news and also find out what was going on out there in the streets and the business since the church had bought it from me. Tina and I went on that helicopter ride. It was nice; it took a lot of fear out of us. We both wanted to go to Florida next, to sit on the white sand beaches, sightsee, and eat some of the best food in the world. We were even going to Disney World. Yeah, two old people having fun, but I wished this was with my wife Leslie.

I got a messed-up phone call. We had to get back home ASAP. Uncle Bobby was dead, my wife's uncle, who helped me with my cabin. We were on the next plane back to Louisville, Kentucky. He showed me the inside hustle. Uncle Bob wasn't all that lonely. He had strippers and a party *barn* on the weekend, with many women in and out—a seventy-three-year-old man acting like he was twenty-two or something. He had money, or should I say got big money. His *funeral* would be at his house, and we would place his body next to my wife's grave.

My wedding was still on for September 12, and Uncle Bob's *funeral* would be within the next two days. His body would be inside his living room, cold but not *embalmed*. It was crazy this way, but at the same time, my health was not well, but we were not telling anyone just yet.

Down South, this was how they did things. Everyone was sad and happy at the same time. My nephew, the pastor, and I took the time to go fishing on the river, drinking some *corn*, laughing, and talking about the Cleveland drama. The pastor was asking too many open questions, like he was up to something. He owed me another $1.2 million for my business, which was doing well as always. My tenants were still upstairs paying rent. The hood still respected that area by not hanging around.

Later, when we went back to the business office, admiring today's catch—not enough fish to sell but enough for tonight's dinner—fish and spaghetti and table white wine, introducing everyone, my family, her family, and the church family felt like family.

I had to pull my nephew to the side. We both heard the pastor being *nervous* when we were talking today on the river. Was he trying to get out of paying us that money, or was he working with the FBI? We couldn't touch him; this was the problem. I pulled my daughter in to talk. I told her what we thought was going on with him. She said, "Daddy, put a wire in their room, and I will stay close to his wife." My nephew agreed. Everything went as planned.

The funeral and my wedding went smoothly. Tina was now Tina Thomas Williams—just "Tina Williams." I liked "Mrs. Williams." We went back out to Disney World to enjoy our trip. My nephew, my brother, and my daughter would handle the pastor and his wife. We couldn't kill them because there were other members here with them, and Cleveland members knew they were all here as well.

We left Cleveland dry and didn't look back. They never said anything in their room, and his wife never talked much. So we gave them a pass but kept an eye on them. My wife now heard a little bit of us talking about the pastor and his wife and what we wanted to do. She asked, "Were we some gangsters?"

I laughed slowly and said, "Yes, we were. At one time, but we retired."

She understood and said, "Out of sight, out of mind. Not my business, honey."

I hugged her and said, "Good girl," and started making love, putting her to sleep.

I called my nephew. He told me he was walking through the strippers' dressing room and found a crack pipe and a small bag of crack. He hit the roof, stopping the club for a few days for everyone to take drug tests. Two failed, but he got rid of everyone and hired all new strippers. No drugs allowed. I couldn't get mad at him because that was our starting rule. Tina and my daughter were mad but, at the same time, respectfully understanding of my nephew's decision. It would be more work to monitor them, but it would be okay. My niece was more of a crybaby type, so we had to keep her out of the deep family drama.

My wife woke up, hair everywhere. She looked good in her sleep. It was time for some breakfast. It was 3:30 a.m., and we were in the best hotel in Disney World. You know me—I wanted steak and eggs. She wanted cheese eggs, grits, mud catfish, two pieces of white toast, strawberry jelly, and coffee. I tipped the man $100.

Tina was about four and a half months pregnant now. Her stomach was getting big, and she was sick all the time. That afternoon, we would be back home in Kentucky. The girls couldn't wait to see what *gifts* we had gotten for them and play with her stomach. My nephew and I were getting together so I could see what was going on with everything inside and out, even my daughter's business. Speaking of my daughter, her news wasn't told yet, so we were setting tonight up for her surprise. My baby, at thirty years old, in front of everyone, *announced* that she was also getting married and having a baby. Her boyfriend was a football player at Kentucky College. He should be here in a while; he was playing a game on TV.

We put it on, watching him run up and down the field. My nephew met him a few times and liked him. He said, "Dude's okay, Uncle." My nephew scared me sometimes because I had turned him into a beast. Truly, he was like my son, and he felt that from me. My daughter did too. She just smiled and said, "It's okay, Daddy, I know." Everyone was very happy about this great news. But deep inside, I wanted to cry. My little girl had grown up on me, and if her mom were here, she would feel the same way. Two babies in the family might bring more joy to life around here—a niece and an aunt growing up together. Wow.

It had been a month and a half since Uncle Bobby's death. The bank just sent a letter to us about Uncle's farm. We had sixty days to come up with $3.1 million, or we could lose the farm. Since I was the head breadwinner and my wife was the oldest, it was my right to keep her blessings alive. This was why I was here. So we all got together at the store for dinner to talk. Everyone needed to be there and needed to be heard, even Tina, since she was now a part of us.

"Okay, everyone is here. I thank you all for coming tonight. Now we all know that the farm was and is a landmark for this family's name and history. Uncle Bob put me under his wing to show me everything that needed to be shown for this to come. Now your sister, my wife, his niece, was his only niece alive who had the heart to run the family business. You other girls are just girls, normal housewife types. Now Uncle's farm has put food on a lot of tables, paid for a lot of bills, and sent children all the way through school. That's what this means—to stick together as one. Anyway, I have a bag that's put up. I have $4 million in cash right now that belongs to Jasmine, Tonya, and Stephanie. My wife and I had this money put up since my robbery in Cleveland. The truth is out now."

Tina looked in shock. "Yes, baby. This is how I made my money—a gangster. And I moved out here because I'm dying soon of cancer like my wife did. I don't have much longer to live anyway. I had made a promise to my wife that I would not tell or give up the money until you all had gotten married and were happy as a family. I see this in each and every one of you. I'm proud to be a part of you all. And nephew, your aunt prayed for our friendship to come this close, which it did. As everything has been given, I will make sure that the nephew, myself, and Jasmine will take it in. Meanwhile, are there any other family issues that need to be addressed?

"Debbie and Linda, my wife's sisters, you two are doing so well with the restaurant. The farm is yours, and everyone will help take care of it. Agreed, right, everyone?"

"No problem," everyone agreed.

"Tina and I will stay at the cabin, which is on the edge of the farm. We both can see each door. I am so glad because there's no way of getting to a hospital in time to have a baby. I want to be in that room that day. I'll be around, just know that." Everyone was laughing.

"Scary-ass nigga," someone joked.

"Yup!"

Tina and my daughter were in the cabin together. It was almost that time. I hired two real live-in nurses to watch them and a doctor with a helicopter on the hospital roof. All of this is my life—my babies. I couldn't sleep. They were doing what they do: eat, cry, and scream at me.

And him, he was right here with me going through it. I liked him, but I told him, "If you misuse my baby just once, I will burn you alive, or I will let her kill you herself."

He looked in fear.

I said, "Don't be afraid. These are real facts. One day, if it's a girl, you will say and feel the same thing."

I heard the helicopter flying over my head. It was that time. We didn't know which was coming; we couldn't go inside. For germs, the nurse and my wife were going toward the helicopter. So I called my nephew to come and get me while Dennis waited on my daughter. My nephew and his wife were here in minutes. He called to order flowers and balloons to be there before she got there. All I knew was that it was twins. Someone called the doctor. The twins would be here in a minute. Man, we were trippin'. It was going to be a boy.

Since Uncle Bob had just bought a new RV, I was going to start and run it for a while and put it behind my cabin so my nephew, Dennis, and I could stay in it while my daughter had my grandbaby. The shotguns were loaded and locked, ready for anything that came. The RV windows would be open so we could hear them. My grandbaby, with her grown self, flew to the hospital to see her cousins. I had two girls, five and a half pounds each. They had to stay until they got all the checkups needed and were eating right.

My daughter's baby was hardheaded; it must be a boy. All the girls were inside. My newborns were inside now. We couldn't go inside to touch or hold them, just look through the window. From here, they looked like me and her but mostly her, and my daughter.

At four o'clock in the morning, her water must have just broken. We had them running through the cabin. Someone called the doctor. The helicopter would be here in a minute. Man, we were trippin'. It was going to be a boy.

I called the hospital to set up the roses and balloons just before she arrived. The flowers would be placed in her room. Someone said it was a girl; we weren't too sure. My nephew had to put the RV in the parking lot in the back. My daughter just came in; the baby was wrapped up and going into another room. My sisters said that the baby needed some oxygen; she wasn't breathing right. A few minutes later, the doctor came out saying that the baby was fine. She weighed seven and a half pounds, and one of her eyes was open. We could see them now.

My daughter was in and out but okay. I held my grandbaby; she held on to my finger and smiled. That's my blood right there. It was time for me and my nephew to leave anyway. The nurse and the doctor had to do some women's things. All the girls were there with her and Dennis. She was in good hands. Now we could go home and have a drink. My wife and the baby were good with a nurse in the cabin. We were going to the club to see what was going on. It was popping.

"Man, all these girls. Can you believe this? I want my babies' names to be Tyesha and Syesha. What's your daughter's name going to be?"

"I don't know," he said just before he passed out again. That's the new daddy thing. We started laughing. Tina might want to name the babies something different.

There were so many women in and out it was hard to keep count, so I was doing this the smart way—out of the way inside the RV, watching TV. There were three newborn babies in that cabin. Wow.

It had been over four days, and everybody was about to go somewhere. Sitting in my special chair, she put the girls down in my arms. One put her hand in my eye, and the other one was reaching for Mommy. So the one in my eye would be named Tyesha, and the other one would be named Syesha. My wife felt so good sitting in my lap. I asked her, "Are you okay with all this? It's not too much to handle, Tina, baby. I'm right with you. Always remember that and make sure that my girls will always know their Daddy's memories."

It had been a month and a half. My daughter had set her wedding date for December 3, 2019. The girls would be two months old by then. Their birthdays were September 23, 2019, and September 27, 2019. That's her baby's birthday. I had time to use Dennis to help bale the hay. I called the county doctor to come and make sure that the animals were not sick and that the meat in the freezer and cooler was okay as well. Then I started to cut up the firewood and cover up the RV.

Time goes fast when you're having fun. Everything was okay with the meats and the animals. Now we just had to clean out the stalls for the horses, chickens, cows, and pigs. My wife's kids were looking at me, laughing. Even though they were little, they were laughing at me—the city man, a farm man, working on a farm. The inside of the house was perfect; hardly anything needed to be done.

I was forgetting something. My daughter's wedding was in the morning. She didn't want hers to be too big. She was still tired from the baby. The live-in nurse she had was coming to help with the baby. That was good. I let him go now and paid him $3,000 for helping me.

After working on the farm and coming in like a man is supposed to, it makes a man feel like a man. You can't hear anything like you do in the city. The air is fresh, and the sky is so dark and bright with the stars and the moon. In Cleveland, you can never be this close to them, as if you can reach out and touch them.

My wife had prepared a candlelight dinner. The fireplace was burning. She was in a silk nightgown. The babies played themselves to sleep. Her six weeks were over.

We talked as I ate my dinner. Once again, I asked her, "Are you happy?" She said yes. I could see the happiness all over her face. I was afraid of leaving her alone.

She said, "Baby, let's take off and go back to Cleveland, to the Cleveland Clinic. They might have an answer for your cancer. Besides, I have never been to Cleveland, Ohio, before."

"Okay, baby," I said.

She kept saying everything would be okay. So I set it up. This time, we took a plane, and my wife and daughter had a ball on the plane, even though they were little.

We landed at Hopkins Airport around 12:30 p.m. on a Wednesday, the same day as my appointment at 4:00 p.m. I had enough time to rent a truck. She liked Kia Souls, so we got a gray four-door, with baby seats—they were extra. We rode down the freeway, and she was amazed by the smell and how the trash was everywhere. We got off at E. Ninth and Chester. Coming up, she saw empty fields, empty old houses, and nothing but people walking around with red lips on most. She asked, "Is this really how Cleveland looks?" She said, "I can smell the death in the air."

We got up to the front door of the Cleveland Clinic. She was deeply touched by how big and empty it looked. I said, "This is the best hospital in the world. The president of the United States comes here."

"Wow," she said.

As we walked through, we saw someone like a singer or rapper with a lot of bodyguards. Tina was trippin'. At my doctor's office, we sat and waited. The doctor had just called me back. He started to explain that there was a breakthrough in medicine for cancer.

I took her all over the place: East Cleveland, Cleveland Heights, Shaker, Downtown. We parked and walked around Public Square and Tower City. I rode around the 200, and we walked around seeing the animals. She loved the city despite the look. I even showed her my old neighborhoods.

Friday came, so we got back to Cleveland Clinic to see my doctor. All the nurses loved my girls everywhere we went. The doctor said that my cancer was gone and that I was the healthy man that Tina and the kids needed around. She hugged me with a face full of tears, saying she—or I should say *they*—loved me. I had tears in my eyes too. I was sixty-three years old and felt like I was sixteen years old. Now it was on; we as a family were about to travel across the world—that is, if Tina allowed it.

We wanted to drive back to Kentucky just to enjoy the nice clear view. The girls slept most of the ride. Tina laid her head on my shoulder, listening to R&B music, which made me feel like the king of the world, which I was.

Getting back, I couldn't wait to tell everyone the good news, even though on the down-low, some wanted the worst. Yeah, things were about to change. So I set up another family meeting at Uncle Bob's house because I wanted to see why I asked the sisters to move there and for everyone else to chip in to feed the animals. The animals hadn't been tended to in days. I could understand how they didn't want to live there, but the animals still needed attention and feeding.

My nephew was too busy. I made that happen to see if he could handle it. In many ways, he had, and I was proud of him, but my money was not in my pocket. Since I was still the primary owner of everything, I temporarily closed everything down. We agreed that everyone should play their part in Uncle Bob's home. If money ruled like this, I would take the business away and sell it. If my wife were alive, she would feel the same damn way. It's crazy; if the animals got sick, we could get sick too. Germs are airborne, and we're right this close by.

I said, "Okay, here's my gun. Do you know how to shoot a gun?" She hurriedly took it, aimed, and barely killed the target, but she hit it nicely. She jumped for joy. The girls were somewhere else, not paying us any attention at all. That was good to know. Now I knew she wasn't afraid of shooting anyone. We took the turkey she had in her hands. The girls were playing, ready for sleep time soon. Tina broke the turkey's neck; it was still alive. Uncle Bob had a big pot outside to boil the wild turkey in. She was happy as hell, and I was happy to see her like this.

First, she cut the neck off, then the legs, and hung it upside down to drain the blood. She looked back at me, saying, "This is what country girls do, honey. I hadn't done this in a long-ass time."

I was like, "Wow, really, I can see that."

"And if you can't help in keeping this farm running, then you won't be doing shit. Everywhere will be closed or sold. This is the first and last time I'm talking about this. If there are any questions, talk to me and Damon. If there's no $50,000 in my father's hands today, then the keys will be… My father shared the good news that his cancer was gone. You all were unhappy, which is good to know because he isn't someone to mess with. I am."

Tina and I sat there with our mouths open like, "Wow, who is that?"

In my head, I thought, *My baby. That's my blood right there. Her mother would have been proud of her for standing up for us and the whole family.*

After the meeting, we asked if we could take the baby with us for a while. She said sure because she had to go home and kick Dennis out anyway. He wasn't going to the NFL. He was caught up in drugs and with a nasty White girl from another strip club downtown.

My daughter was mad as hell. She thought that what I had asked was understood. So yes, we needed a meeting. She said, "Like my father at Uncle Bob's house, I am going to pull back and listen to what's being said." My daughter meant it. I paid a lot of money for a family dream and history to let it go to waste. No, I don't think so.

Everyone came into the house, looking around in fear. I was sitting in the corner with my family, my girls playing with each other. No one said a word toward us, like usual. I told my wife, "Shit's about to hit the fan."

My daughter came in. She kicked it with her sisters and asked Tina to hold our grandbaby. All three were having a ball together like they knew they were family. Words started coming out. She asked everyone if they had anything really before my parents asked them to come to Cleveland to put their hands up. No hands went up.

"What the fuck were you before all this went down?" Still no word.

"Okay," she said. "This is why we meet. My parents kept their word and blessed you all. The only thing in return is that everyone helps keep the farm up and running. This house is putting food on the tables and money in your pockets."

I, Tina, and my babies started walking through the tall grass to check on the animals. Tina said, "Baby, you can let them out to run and graze. Besides, the grass needs to be eaten down."

So I did. They were happy like humans. Everything was okay. We walked around sightseeing. The girls saw a family of deer. They were happy, pointing and trying their best to talk. I noticed right between some woods stood a house of some sort. I told them to stay back and let me go and see what it was and how long it had been there.

As I walked, I began to see a lot of different things like traps, people's footsteps, and ropes on trees. But the building had been empty for years. I wondered if Uncle had had any kinds of problems with this. I went inside the building. It appeared to be an old Baptist church. Was this part of my wife's family history?

I got back to Tina and the kids. They were okay. We continued walking toward the cabin. Tina noticed a wild turkey, a big black one, ahead. She wanted to try to kill it.

Sitting here watching her cook this turkey over an open fire smells so good. I called my nephew to see if he knew anything about that building or church at the back of Uncle's house. He said this was the first time he had heard about it too, so I called Sister Linda, the second oldest. She said the same thing. My daughter called, asking if everything was okay and how the baby was doing. I handed the phone to my wife so the girls could talk.

I went inside my secret hole in the floor, getting my AR and a few clips out, along with two bulletproof vests for us. Everyone was going to be here tomorrow afternoon so we could walk through and look around. Tina's turkey had the whole farm smelling good. I was amazed; it was like deep frying it in grease.

To keep myself busy, I checked my fishing rods to make sure they were good. Tina loves fishing too. The girls were asleep on the floor in plain sight. Tina and I talked about finding the building. It looked old, but the footsteps seemed a few weeks old.

It was getting dark soon and hot. The animals looked fine. I gave Tina a 9 mm and an AR, both loaded, and told her I was going to walk around to check our surroundings. Uncle's house was locked up well, the motion lights were working, and the fence around the farm looked okay. But it felt like some eyes were watching me, so I walked slowly with my hands tight on my AR. The cows and horses were busy eating, which was good. Tina's turkey was done, and dinner was ready. I was hungry enough to eat a horse.

Tina asked, "Can I too, '101'?"

While she prepared the table, I thought I saw something like a human move on the hill. Maybe my mind was playing games. I told Tina, and her words were, "It's always spirits that come out at night."

I sat there, a little confused, and asked, "Tina, baby, are you okay?"

She said, "Baby, come and eat."

We sat and ate. The girls woke up from the smell of the food. They were now two years old, with big teeth, and calling my name and their mother's name, "Mom's." It sounded funny to me because it was said in a country tongue.

Tina's food tasted good. The turkey was juicy. My grandbaby jumped up and went to Tina's side, saying, "Eat, eat." Tyesha was awake now, and soon all of them were awake. That meant playtime and cartoons all night. I lay on the couch and watched them drive me crazy as usual.

At 10:00 p.m. here in Cleveland, it was 8:30 p.m., I think. Tina was kicking it with the girls. She saw something from the corner of her eye: a light moving through the woods far up on the hill. It was too far to walk to in a short time or to shoot at, so we watched it go in and out. It stayed on that hill. Maybe a neighbor was looking around their land. "It's nothing, I'm sure," I said.

While the girls were being girls, I got a few hours of sleep. I always woke before 5:00 a.m. anyway. I sat there quietly, turned on the news, smoked a Newport, and drank some tea, listening for anything like escapes from jails. Nothing was reported. I woke Tina up with a soft kiss and put her on the couch with her guns, telling her I was outside checking things out. So far, everything seemed okay around my cabin, the RV, and my truck.

I called my nephew and told him to stop at city hall or the bank and get his uncle's deed to the farm. After that, everyone could come up here. By 8:30 a.m., we were all there with guns. There were about thirty of us. The animals were accounted for and okay. We started inside the house, checking everything. We left all the women in the house to check for any paperwork about the property too. It was said that Uncle owned 135 acres of land here. That meant no one around should be there without being on this paper or map.

We started around the barn, walking slowly, avoiding trap holes. I took them to the building I had found. They were tripping now, seeing the ropes hanging from the trees and the footprints in the dirt.

We searched all around the building but found no signs of life, just a funny smell like rotten meat. I found some old Bibles sitting on benches. They were so old it was crazy.

As we started walking away, we noticed a graveyard ahead of us. The grass had overgrown it. There were at least ten graves, with dates from the 1200s to 1931. The names were Wallace.

I called up to the house to check on everybody. They were good. Nothing was found except some pork chops and rice for lunch. That sounded really good at that moment. My nephew suggested putting up some motion detectors and cameras to see what it was. *A human? Okay, spirits*, I thought. Tina was talking about spirits earlier. Whatever it was, it could be dealt with, trust that.

Nephew and the others said at the same time, "Do you guys feel that?"

I said, "What?"

"Someone's watching us."

"Where?"

"Back there, by the tote building."

"What is it, and what the fuck was that smell?"

Right after that, a rock was thrown over our heads, a nice-sized one. We stopped quickly, making sure everyone was okay. My phone rang. The girls were all at the window, saying that a man just threw that rock from that building and was on the roof. We headed back fast, guns ready. Fresh footprints were right there, size 13 in shoes. My wife's uncle Bob was tall; he was six feet four and 265 pounds, a big man. Maybe we were playing with a ghost or something. We followed the smell into the woods. It was hard to find anything, but we kept looking.

I said, "I'm not the police type, you all know this, but we might have to call them for help. Whatever it is, it's quick and strong. The question is, what does it want, and why is it staying around?"

My nephew and I decided to burn this building. Everyone, even the girls, agreed in fear. My nephew and I started back to the barn for gasoline. We heard a tree break. I fired a warning shot. Nothing. We kept going.

Whatever it was lived there, we guessed strongly. It was trying to protect its home. The girls asked in fear if it was human. In the background, I heard the babies saying, "Dad, Dad." They were looking out the windows in everyone's arms.

We set the fire. It spread fast. Dirt surrounded it, so it couldn't spread to the trees. There was no wind blowing, just perfect. It smelled really bad, like human flesh or some animals burning. The police called, asking if there was anything else. A few minutes after that call, we heard a loud "roar." A big blast burst through the door, a figure on fire running fast. It was the biggest thing we had ever seen. We started shooting, unloading our guns, chasing this thing. It was unbelievable. What the hell was it? It headed toward the riverbed. Looking up, we saw helicopters—US Army, police, sheriffs, news crews. We were like, "What the hell?"

All the women came running out, looking around. Even the animals were tripping and running around. The police asked us to go back into the house and wait. They started answering our questions about what it was. How long had it been around here? What was the history of this farm? Secrets were being told. We listened intently.

A week later, we received a check for $1,000,000 to keep quiet.

In a struggle, try to make a change to get out of the gang.